CAVE
OF
FALLING
WATER

D1115093

CAVE
OF
FALLING
WATER

✣

Janice Ovecka

illustrated by
David Kanietakeron Fadden

THE NEW ENGLAND PRESS
Shelburne, Vermont

© 1992 by Janice Ovecka
All Rights Reserved
Printed in the United States of America
First Edition

For additional copies or for a catalog of our other New England
titles, please write:

The New England Press
P.O. Box 575
Shelburne, VT 05482

Ovecka, Janice, 1956-
    Cave of Falling Water / Janice Ovecka ; illustrated by David
Kanietakeron Fadden. -- 1st ed.
        p. cm.
    Summary: For each of three girls growing up in different periods
of Vermont's history, one Abenaki, one colonial white, and one a
modern girl, a cave serves as an important refuge.
    ISBN 0-933050-98-4 : $9.95
    [1. Caves--Fiction. 2. Vermont--Fiction. 3. Abenaki Indians--
Fiction. 4. Indians of North America--Fiction.] I. Fadden, David
Kanietakeron, ill. II. Title.
PZ7.0944Cav 1992
[Fic]--dc20   92-56713
                                                   CIP
                                                    AC

Contents

——— ❖ ———

*Dedicated to the most dynamic force in the history of
Vermont, her children—
and most especially, my children
Angela, Elaine, and David.*

Acknowledgments

The author most gratefully acknowledges the help of
Dr. William Haviland, University of Vermont;
Jill R. Corliss, Lothrop School, Pittsford, Vt.;
Sandra Conway, Maclure Library, Pittsford, Vt.;
and the staff of The New England Press, Inc.

Woni

———— ✤ ————

*T*he firelight reflected off the walls of the lodge as the Storyteller spoke in deep, soft tones. The expressions of the people gathered around the fire were varied. The babies and young children, long asleep, snuggled in their mother's arms, and the older children, captivated by the Storyteller's words, wore eager, interested faces. The adults, remembering the first time they had heard the story, were smilingly reminiscent.

"And that is why the maple tree loses her leaves in the dead of the year and is reborn in the spring." With those words, the spell was broken and the gathering dispersed. The women hustled the protesting children off to bed, while the men stayed by the fire, speaking in low voices.

1

Woni snuggled down into her warm furs. She looked at her brother sleeping next to her and thought of her friend Falling Water, who, in times past, had occupied that spot. As she looked around the lodge, she saw many empty places and remembered many faces, who, like Falling Water, had fallen victim to the Evil Spirit that brought the disease.

"So many dead," thought Woni. "What will become of our people?" As she drifted off to sleep, she thought of Falling Water and wondered if she would ever stop missing her.

Morning came soon in that early springtime. Woni awoke and stretched, yawning as the mists of her dreams gave way to the daylight. The lodge was warm, the men were gone, and Woni heard the murmur of the women cooking and feeding their babies and urging young children out of bed.

She got up and dressed quickly. Her aunt combed and plaited her thick hair for her, chattering away in the manner of the squirrel, for which she had been named.

"How can my aunt be so cheerful," wondered Woni, "when her husband is dead with two children beside him?" Everywhere she looked, her people appeared normal. Only the dark hoods of the widows gave any outward sign of the great tragedy that had befallen them. But the tragedy that the sickness had brought was real, still lurking just behind the eyes of all those who had survived.

"We are not ill, but we still suffer," she thought.

Woni picked up her basket and stepped through the doorway of the lodge. She looked around the clearing and saw a handful of hastily improvised homes—not the bustling, handsome community it once had been. When the disease spread to their village, Woni's family had left their warm winter lodges in the valley and sought refuge in their summer dwellings. Here on the mountain, winter was not kind, and the appearance of spring brought mud and cold rain and sudden, unexpected frosts.

The community's food supply was dwindling, and every morning Woni and the other young women and girls gathered ferns and early spring greens for their dinner. The men hunted the sparse game, while the older women gathered the remaining maple sap and boiled it for the sugar.

The breeze of this morning held a promise of summer to come, and Woni's spirits lifted a little. She decided to gather ferns on the ridge behind the clearing. A small creek ran through the gorge on the other side. "Perhaps the water-plants are big enough to eat," she thought.

She soon gathered a basketful of the delicious greens and sat down on a boulder to rest. The sun was warm and the creek gurgled as it rushed by next to her. Woni nibbled on the young ferns, delighted by their crunchiness after a long winter of dried venison and fish.

A twig snapped behind her and Woni swung around. A young man was picking his way down the side of the gorge. He was tall, his thick dark hair caught in a woven band. His bow hung loosely in his right hand, but Woni knew that he would have an arrow at the ready in an instant if a foolish animal crossed his path. His name was simply the Hawk, and he had provided more game for the village in his seventeen years than many grown men had in their lifetimes.

"Ah, ah, ah," teased Woni. "What kind of woodcraft is that? You sound like a bull moose charging through the trees."

The Hawk smiled. "I snapped that twig on purpose. I didn't want you to accuse me of sneaking up on you." He took some of the young ferns out of Woni's basket and ate them with relish

"So where have you been this time?" asked Woni.

"Around," he said. "How are things in the village?"

Woni's face darkened. "About the same. So empty."

"You feel her loss greatly," the Hawk said gently.

Woni nodded. The Hawk's hard face softened with sympathy. "I miss her too," he said. "Falling Water was a special person. There will never be another." He shook his head. "Can you imagine what she would say to us right now?"

"She would probably push you in the water," said Woni with a sad smile.

"Well, she might try," he said, puffing himself up with exaggerated pride. "But she certainly would not succeed. Come on—I want to show you something."

The Hawk crept across the boulders, Woni following silently behind. Their deerskin moccasins made no sound, and they both moved quickly, with the easy grace that came of spending a lifetime on the mountain.

Finally the Hawk stopped and as Woni came up behind him, he pointed to an opening in the rocks. The hole was a little more than two feet across. The Hawk wriggled in, motioning for Woni to follow. Woni crouched down and crawled through the opening.

As her eyes adjusted to the dark, Woni saw that she was in a small cave, just high enough for the Hawk to stand erect without hitting his head. Woni looked around eagerly.

"What a wonderful cave!" she exclaimed.

"I found it just yesterday," said the Hawk. "I thought at first it was an animal den, but there is no animal sign at all. This cave has never been used before."

"Perhaps you were the first to find it. Imagine it being here since Odzihozo created it, just waiting for you to find it," Woni said. "Now we shall have to call you 'Finder of Lost Caves.'"

"'Hawk' is much easier to say," he replied with a smile. He looked around. "Falling Water would have loved this place."

"Yes, she would," agreed Woni. "She would have found a name for it, probably something very extravagant."

"Why don't we name it?" asked the Hawk. "We'll name it Cave of Falling Water and dedicate it to her memory."

"That's a wonderful idea," said Woni.

The Hawk closed his eyes and held his arms out from his sides, palms up.

"I, the Hawk, name this place Cave of Falling Water

6

and dedicate it to Falling Water forever." He brought his hands together across his chest and bowed his head.

Woni bowed her head and thought of Falling Water. She thought of all her people—those who had died, and those left behind to grieve.

After a moment she spoke. "Hawk," she said softly, as he lifted his head and opened his eyes. "Why don't we really dedicate it to Falling Water?"

"What do you mean?"

"Well, in those last days when Falling Water and the others were dying, we were not able to bury them all. My grandfather made us leave them behind, and we never said good-bye." Woni's eyes glimmered with tears. "I know it was so that the Evil Spirit did not catch us and give us the disease too, but I can't stop thinking about all our loved ones going into the afterlife alone and without food or warm furs. Perhaps if we create a burial chamber here for Falling Water, her spirit will find it."

"She would have been my wife," the Hawk said after a long silence. "She should have had the grandest burial of any woman." He turned to Woni. "Yes, we will do this. We will make this her burial chamber." Abruptly, he turned and left the cave.

Woni followed him out, and the two retrieved Woni's basket of greens. They walked silently back to the village until the screech of a hawk overhead broke the silence.

The Hawk looked up at the bird as it circled in the sky.

"Oh, yes, my friend," he said with a smile, "you are truly a magnificent being."

Woni shook her head. "So you're talking to hawks again, are you? The women are already talking about you as the next shaman."

"I am no wise man," the Hawk said with a snort. "I merely see what is there for anyone to see."

"And what do you see, Hawk-eyes?" Woni asked.

The Hawk stopped in the path. "I see that our old way of life is vanishing and that nothing will be as it was."

Woni's eyes were troubled. "Why do you say that?"

"Look," he said, opening the leather pouch at his waist and drawing out a handful of arrowheads. "My grandfather used arrowheads of flint, carved from the rocks of the earth, as did his grandfather before him. But now the hunters use these arrowheads made of metal, obtained from the white-skinned traders in exchange for our furs. The art of carving arrowheads is almost lost, and we grow ever more reliant on these traders for everything, even the beads with which we adorn our clothing." The Hawk replaced the arrowheads in his pouch and turned to Woni. His eyes were harsh and his mouth grim.

"I have seen these white traders," he said. "Not only do they have metal arrowheads, but they have weapons that shoot from long distances that can drop a bear in its tracks. I have seen this with my own eyes, and I wonder how we can fight these people."

"There is no need to fight them," said Woni. "There is plenty of food and land for everyone. Our only enemies are the Iroquois, and they have not attacked us for a very long time. Why should we have to fight the white man?"

"You are too kind, Little Otter," said the Hawk, brushing his hand over her cheek. "I do not really think they will have to fight us. Our numbers are few and growing fewer from the disease. Yet the white man's magic makes him strong, and every day more traders appear. They have even brought their own shamans with them, men in black robes who they say have power over the disease. They talk of a new god, and many of our people have listened. No, Woni, our lives are changing. Soon these white men will take over our land, and our people will have nowhere to go. Nowhere to hunt."

"Surely it will not be that bad," said Woni.

"You are very young," he said, taking her hand in his. "I can only hope that you are right and that our people will continue to live in peace."

"I may be young," said Woni with a smile, "but even I know that change is part of life. Perhaps you are growing too old to change."

The Hawk looked affronted. He scowled at Woni, but then he tilted his head back and laughed heartily.

"Perhaps you are right. And since I am so ancient, you can carry your own basket." With that, the two turned and walked back to the village.

The village bustled with activity. The women gathered around a large fire in the center of the clearing while groups of men who had returned from the hunt prepared the meat for smoking. Old men squatted in the doorways of the lodges, gossiping and smoking their pipes, while small children dashed here and there in a lively game of tag. Everyone was busy except for the very young—even the older children had their duties to perform.

Woni took her basket of greens to her aunt, who was preparing a stew, then joined the group of women at the fire. They were making sugar, boiling down maple sap they had collected until it crystallized. Woni scooped up a small patch of lingering snow, and her mother poured a thin stream of the sap onto it. Woni ate it, making a wry face as the confection stuck to her teeth, gluing them together. Her mother laughed as Woni labored to move her jaw.

"That should make your teeth strong," she said.

"Not if they fall out," Woni said with a grin when she had finally swallowed the candy.

Woni held her snow-chilled hands out to the fire. She noticed the women were using a metal pot to boil the sap in, instead of the old birchbark vessels they used in the past.

"Maybe the Hawk is right," she thought. "We're even using the white man's metal goods to cook in."

Woni's grandmother, White Feather, approached the group. "You know that sugar will have no flavor," she admonished. "That iron pot will sour it."

"Bah," replied Woni's mother. "The sugar will be fine. Besides, the iron pot is much faster."

The women were soon engaged in a lively discussion

of sugar making, and Woni turned away, uninterested in the finer points of sap boiling. She crossed the clearing to her family's lodge, and, lifting the heavy deerskin from across the doorway, she went inside.

The interior was dark, the only light being the soft red glow from the fires at either end of the rectangular long-house. Around the stone rings that enclosed the fires stood large clay pots, hand-made with snug-fitting lids. These pots contained the group's food: smoked meat and fish, ground maize, beans, nuts, maple sugar, and cakes made of ground venison and berries called pemmican. Baskets of dried fruit and herbs were kept a small distance away from the fires, but their aroma filled the air of the snugly built lodge. Food gathering and growing were the community's main occupations, so all foodstuffs were carefully prepared and stored. All members of the group shared equally in the bounty of the land so that no one went hungry.

Beds of soft furs were arranged along the outer walls of the birchbark-covered lodge. On the coldest nights, these furs were brought near the fire, but they were placed out of the way during the day. Woni went to her bed, a mound of soft deerskins with a covering of beaver pelts. Her pillow was a rabbit fur that had been carefully tanned by her mother many years before. Next to her pillow was a woven basket that contained all of Woni's personal possessions. These were few—a cornhusk doll, made by her grandmother and dressed in a tiny deer-skin robe, a soft leather pouch filled with shells and pretty stones, a long necklace of beads, shells, and feathers, and her light summer moccasins. Soon, as the weather improved, her winter leggings would be put away in the basket.

Behind the basket, near the wall, stood a small clay pot. Woni knelt and drew the pot toward her. She lifted the lid, and inside there were hundreds of kernels of maize, or Indian corn. She ran her fingers through it and thought back to the previous autumn, to the day she and Falling Water had harvested the plot of maize they had carefully tended all summer.

Woni sighed. It seemed so long ago. She and Falling Water had worked hard, but it had seemed like play as they laughed over Falling Water's outrageous story of the Maize Prince and the Magic Toad. The sun had been warm and bright, and they had sung and laughed and talked of next year's crop. But now Falling Water was gone, and only the hard kernels of maize were left.

The next morning Woni awoke early, and after her small breakfast she hurried through her chores. She shook out her sleeping furs and made her bed. She then took the bones left from a squirrel her aunt had stewed the day before and carefully buried them outside the clearing, reciting the ritual prayers to the animal's spirit, thanking him and apologizing so that he would not be offended. Then she grabbed her gathering basket, placed the clay pot inside, and hurried to the small creek.

At first Woni could not find the little cave, but soon she recognized a group of boulders that formed a series of steps down the side of the gorge, and she followed them to the mouth of the cave.

The inside of the cave was much brighter today, and Woni realized that the sun was shining almost directly into the opening. She could make out the stone walls much better than the day before. At the back of the cave she found a little niche in the wall, so she placed the clay pot on the ledge and knelt.

"Why, it looks as if that ledge were made especially for my pot of maize," she thought in wonder. Indeed, the pot looked as if it belonged, a part of the cave, now making it complete.

Woni stepped outside and searched among the boulders for a hard rock. She found the one she wanted, sharply pointed at one end, the other end smooth and flat. Then she selected another rock, slightly larger, and returned to the cave.

Kneeling by the wall near the opening, she placed the sharp, pointed rock at an angle to the rough wall and struck it repeatedly with the larger stone. She kept hammering, and soon designs appeared under her moving chisel.

Woni was absorbed in her work when a shadow fell across the opening, blocking the light. She spun around to see the Hawk coming through the opening.

"What are you doing?" he demanded.

"And good morning to you too," said Woni. "Since you asked, I'm carving pictures for Falling Water."

"Pictures?" he asked, perplexed.

"Yes," replied Woni. "We used to always draw pic-

tures in the dirt with a stick, remember? But then the
rain would wash them away. I want these pictures to
last, so I am drawing them in the rock."

The Hawk made no reply to this explanation, but he
studied Woni's pictures carefully. "That must be you
and Falling Water," he said. "But what's that thing
overhead?"

"That's you, silly," said Woni. "That's supposed to be
a hawk. See the talons?"

"Pretty small hawk," he said, but he made no other comment as Woni worked the stone.

Soon the sun had moved away from the opening, and it was too dark to work. The two left the cave, and the Hawk disappeared into the forest. Woni gathered more greens and returned to the village.

Woni spent the rest of the day helping her mother and the other women as they wrapped the finished maple sugar for storage. When the work was complete, Woni joined her aunt as she scraped a deerhide in preparation for tanning. The two scraped away flesh and fat with dull knives, taking care not to tear the hide. Woni worked silently, half listening to her aunt as she chattered away.

Suddenly her aunt broke off in the middle of a sentence, and Woni looked up, startled. Her aunt was staring, a tense expression on her face, and Woni turned around. A sudden hush fell on the community as two strangers stepped out of the forest. An old man and a young girl stood warily at the edge of the clearing.

The Hawk was the first to reach them, the other men close behind. He stood in their path, blocking the way, and studied them silently.

The old man had scraggly white hair and a large nose that jutted from his lined face. He wore a deerskin tunic, embroidered lavishly, but his breeches were of a strange fabric, and on his feet, instead of moccasins, he wore boots—white man's boots. He was travel-stained and weary, and he leaned heavily on his carved walking stick.

The girl was young, about Woni's age, not a child but not yet a woman. She was wearing white man's boots also, but her dress was deerskin. Around her neck she wore a chain of metal from which hung a silver cross that gleamed in the late afternoon sunlight. As the Hawk looked more closely at her face, he saw that it was covered with red pockmarks. He stepped back swiftly and raised his arm, as if to ward off evil.

"Do not be afraid," spoke the old man. "She has had the disease, but she has been cured."

"Cured!" scoffed the Hawk. "No one can cure this disease. No, do not step closer," he said as the man advanced toward him.

"It is true," the old man said. "The priests, the Blackrobes, have cured her. Could she have walked all the way from Odanak if she were ill?"

The men murmured and the Hawk spoke. "Odanak? You have come from the white men, then. What do you want with us? Or do you come to give us the disease again?" he said bitterly.

"I swear to you she is cured. See her face? The scars are healing."

The Hawk looked closely at the girl. She stood tall, and as he met her eyes, she glared at him for a moment, then lowered her gaze. True, she did not appear ill— perhaps the Blackrobes did have power over the disease as he had heard.

The old man spoke. "Why are you so hostile? Is it not the custom of our people to give shelter to travelers? We come in peace and you treat us as enemies. I am Francois de la Griffe, once known as Blackclaw, and this is my daughter's daughter, Marie. I have come to find my family. I have heard that my sister Redwing married a member of the Bear clan, and I have come in search of her."

Woni's grandmother, White Feather, stepped forward. "My brother's wife was named Redwing, and she spoke of a brother who left their clan and went away. But she has been dead many seasons, and her husband with her."

The old man's face fell. "I am too late," he said softly.

"How do we know you are this Blackclaw? You could be a spy, sent by our enemy," spoke out one man, angrily.

"Enough!" The clan's leader, Roaring Bear, stepped forward. "Blackclaw is right. Have we forgotten who we are that we should badger two strangers in such a manner? I apologize," he said with a small bow to the couple. "We have suffered much. We are few and vulnerable, and so we are wary of strangers. But come"—he beckoned—"we will give you shelter and food. Tonight we will hold a council." He turned, and the women led the two away to eat and rest.

Woni and her aunt had not moved, but now Woni turned and watched as her aunt sank to the ground, her hands over her face. Woni knelt and put her arms around the older woman as she began to cry.

"It's not fair! My husband and babies have been taken from me, and this girl lives!" she cried out.

Woni said nothing. She held her aunt as she rocked

back and forth. She had no words of comfort, none for her aunt, none for herself.

The council was held in the largest lodge. The entire village gathered around the fire. It might have been a festive occasion, but an undercurrent of tension rippled among the people. Some, like Woni's aunt, were openly hostile toward the two strangers, while others welcomed them as long-lost relatives.

As Woni ate the freshly roasted venison, she watched the strangers. The old man was engulfed by a crowd of people, regaling them with his life's story. The young girl, though, sat apart and nibbled dully at her food, eyes downcast. Occasionally she looked up furtively at the gathering. Woni thought she looked angry and defiant, as if she were daring someone, anyone, to approach her. Then the girl looked directly at Woni for a moment, and Woni glimpsed a sad, frightened, and very lonely young girl.

"Poor thing," murmured Woni. She felt a surge of sympathy for her, until she remembered the spots on her face. "I don't dare go near her," she thought. But another voice inside her said, "But what if she is cured? She is wearing the white man's charm, is she not? How would you feel to be an outcast as she is?"

Woni rose halfway to her feet, intending to go to the girl, then caught sight of her aunt's warning look. Woni sighed and resumed her seat. "My aunt knows what is in my mind," she thought.

Roaring Bear clapped his hands once, and the people

took their places around the fire. Woni noticed with a shock that the people were divided into two factions, those wishing to turn the strangers away, and those welcoming them. It was unusual to see such division within the community. "We have more to fear than the white man," she thought.

Roaring Bear spoke. "We have received into our midst two strangers. Some think they should be welcomed as is our tradition. Others say they are spies and bear the Evil Spirit. First, we will hear the story of he who calls himself Blackclaw."

The old man rose and gathered an old cloak around his shoulders as if the garment were the robe of a chief.

"I am Blackclaw, the third son of my parents and brother to she who was called Redwing. When I was young, I had no love of hunting or fishing but preferred to trade with other nations. When the white man came to my land, I left my clan and lived among these traders. There were many of our people who did this, as the white men were very generous with us. My name was changed to Francois de la Griffe, and I learned the white man's language and his ways. I traded among them and prospered. I married and my wife bore me one daughter. My daughter preferred the ways of our people, though, so when she died she made me promise that I would take Marie to live among my relatives." He pointed to the young girl, and all stared at her. She flushed under the gaze of the people, making the spots on her face stand out lividly.

"My daughter died of the disease, but the Blackrobes were able to save my granddaughter from death, as you can see. They have said that she is strong and that in time the spots will fade from her face. Believe me, I would not knowingly bring disease to my sister's clan. I only ask that you accept us as your people. I am still a good trader and can obtain much for you in exchange for your furs. My granddaughter has been taught all of the duties of a young woman. Whatever you decide, we thank you for your kind hospitality." He bowed to his audience and sat down.

Roaring Bear said to White Feather, "Is this indeed the brother of Redwing?"

"Redwing often spoke of her brother. Can you tell us why you are called Blackclaw?" White Feather asked.

Blackclaw stood and held out his right hand. The little finger was twisted, and at the end, instead of a fingernail, there was a claw, like the talon of a hawk. "When I was young, my finger was smashed in an accident and the fingernail grew into a claw," he said, as the audience gasped.

White Feather nodded. "It is as Redwing said. I believe that this is my brother's wife's brother."

The Hawk sprang up. "How can we be sure you are not a spy?" he demanded.

"I cannot prove I am not a spy," admitted Blackclaw. "I can only ask that you believe me. Would a spy travel with a young girl? Would a spy tell you openly that he had come from the white man's settlement?"

"This is true," said another man, on the other side of the fire. "We cannot suspect every traveler we meet of spying. Soon we will be accusing even the birds of the air." Some tittered, and the Hawk flushed angrily.

"What of that charm on her neck?" a woman spoke up, pointing at the girl. "What if she is under a spell?"

"That is the symbol of the white man's god," said Blackclaw.

"Then you are a believer," she said. "And the girl too?"

"Yes, we are believers in God, as the white man calls him," said Blackclaw.

"Are you here to turn us away from Odzihozo and the other gods of our ancestors?" persisted the woman.

Blackclaw smiled. "The foreign traders taught me more of this world that we all share, and when the Blackrobes came they taught me more about their god. I came to understand that we are all created by one Great Spirit. The Blackrobes brought me a fuller understanding of God, but I am a simple man and cannot explain these things well. I can only share what I believe with those who wish to know more."

The woman looked at him searchingly and nodded and sat down. The people murmured among themselves, some nodding, some shaking their heads.

Roaring Bear stood up again. "Now it is time to vote. Shall Blackclaw and his granddaughter be permitted to stay?"

One by one, the people raised their hands. As Woni raised hers, she looked over at the Hawk. He did not raise his hand but stared into the fire. Woni surveyed the rest of the group. A clear majority indicated that the couple could stay. Woni breathed a glad sigh of relief.

The crowd all began talking at once, and Roaring Bear embraced Blackclaw as a brother. Marie remained in her place—no one had approached her at all. Then a voice rang out over the tumult.

"But what of the girl? Is she truly cured?" It was Woni's aunt, casting an accusing finger at Marie.

The crowd fell silent. Roaring Bear looked at the shaman, Crowsbeak, and nodded.

Crowsbeak grabbed a torch and lit it from the fire. He walked slowly to Marie and stood before her, the torch bathing her with light. Crowsbeak looked closely at her face, and her eyes, once defiant, fell under his stare.

"Hold out your hands," he said, and she extended them, turning them over for him to inspect. He gingerly touched her wrist, feeling her heart beating clear and strong.

"Open your mouth," he said sharply, and thrust the torch closer. She did as instructed, barely flinching as the fire swept close to her face.

Then Crowsbeak slowly circled around her, sniffing, smelling for the tell-tale signs of disease—the stench of corruption and rotting flesh. He came to a stop in front of her and looked into her eyes. This time she met his gaze directly.

Crowsbeak turned to Roaring Bear and nodded. "She is cured," he said.

Noise erupted again in the lodge. Woni looked at her aunt, who stood and stared at Marie for a moment, then turned away. Woni walked resolutely over to Marie.

"I am Wonakake, but everyone calls me Woni," she said with a tentative smile.

"I am called Marie" was the other girl's unsmiling response.

"Mah-wee . . . Maaah-wee" said Woni, struggling with the awkward sounds of the foreign tongue. "I will never say it right," she said, dismayed.

A smile broke out on Marie's face. She laughed, and

the ice was broken. "You will soon get it right," she said. "The white men say our language is impossible to learn also."

"Hah," snorted Woni. "Anyone who can garble their words like that should find our language easy."

The two smiled at each other, and Woni felt a bond of friendship forming. "Why don't you bring your furs over to our fire?" she suggested. "Your grandfather will probably join our clan." Marie nodded agreement, and Woni made room for Marie's bed next to hers. The two settled down to talk.

Marie pointed to Woni's aunt. "Why does she hate us?" she asked.

"She still grieves for her husband and children," said Woni. "She is resentful that the Evil Spirit has taken them. But don't worry, she is really a very warm and loving person. She will soon come to accept you."

"I suppose the disease took a lot of your people," said Marie.

Woni nodded. "Every family lost someone. My baby brother died, and also my friend, Falling Water."

Marie shook her head slowly. "My mother was the first to die in the village. The Blackrobes said it was not an Evil Spirit, but God who wanted her in heaven. I cannot understand it. I guess He did not want me. Not yet, anyway."

Woni smiled. "I'm glad your god spared you. I still don't understand why Falling Water had to die. The Hawk says maybe she was so good that the Evil Spirit was jealous and took her. I just don't know."

"Which one is the Hawk?" asked Marie.

Woni pointed to the fire where the Hawk sat, talking with the men.

"Oh, yes," said Marie. "He thinks we are spies."

"He is worried about our future. He thinks the white man may make war on us."

"He is right to be worried," said Marie, and Woni looked at her in alarm. "Oh, I don't think the white man will attack us," she reassured Woni. "But the future will hold many changes for our people. More and more white men are coming and bringing their families. They are forming permanent towns. The white men called the French are our friends, and they have been very good to us so far. But even so, our way of life will change."

Woni and Marie talked on about many things before the fire died down and sleep overtook them. Woni fell asleep thinking how nice it was to have a friend to talk to again.

Woni rose early and slipped out past the sleeping Marie. She made her way to the creek and crawled into the cave. In the gloom, she realized that the Hawk was already there, sitting silently on the floor.

He looked up at Woni. "I thought perhaps you would be too busy with your new friend to come here," he said bitterly.

"Oh, no," said Woni. "Marie could never take the place of Falling Water. You know that," she scolded. "You also know that Falling Water would want us to go on with life and make new friends. She was always the first to greet a stranger."

"Yes, you are right," admitted the Hawk. "But I still don't trust that Marie or her grandfather."

"Does it help to know that she shares your distrust of the white man?"

"Oh, really?" The Hawk sounded uninterested, but Woni knew she had given him food for thought.

Woni knelt at her rock drawings and began chiseling. "How much more will you do?" the Hawk asked.

"I think after this picture of Falling Water lying down, I will be finished," she said.

Woni worked silently, and then, indeed, she was finished. She sat back on her heels and surveyed her work—the pictures of herself and Falling Water and the Hawk.

"Even in the midst of all this talk of change, at least there will be something permanent," she said at last.

"And what is that?" asked the Hawk.

"This cave," she said simply. "Long it has stood here, since the dawn of time, and long will it endure. Even if our people vanish forever, the cave will remain. The spirit of Falling Water will dwell here and bring peace and tranquility forever."

"Yes," the Hawk said, laying his hands on Woni's shoulders. "The Cave of Falling Water will stand until the end of time."

Mattie

———— ✤ ————

Mattie lifted the canvas sacking that covered the doorway of the cabin and peeked out. Good—no one in sight. She ducked through and ran to the edge of the rough log cabin and cautiously looked around the corner. She could hear the ring of her father's ax and her mother's voice barking at the plow horse, but they were both over the rise, out of sight of the cabin. She hitched up her skirts and ran through the clearing to the woods. She ran up a tiny path that climbed through the trees until she was sure she could not be seen from the pasture. She sat down on a rock to catch her breath.

Oh, it felt good to be out of that cabin! She drank in the fresh air, grateful to feel its warmth. Spring had finally come to stay, and Mattie felt a sudden urge to move, to stretch her cramped limbs and dance in the sunshine.

She sprang to her feet and whirled around, her woolen cloak falling to the earth, her skirts ballooning out from her legs. Then, the frenzy over, she collapsed, giggling, to the ground. Wouldn't Miss Metcalfe of Miss Metcalfe's Academie for Fine Young Ladyes be shocked! She would purse her dry lips and say, "Martha Hardwicke, fine young ladies do not indulge in such wanton behavior. You must mend your ways, or you'll come to a bad end!" But Miss Metcalfe was far away, and Mattie was free—free to do as she pleased, for who was there to see or even care what she did?

Mattie picked up her cloak and, throwing it over her shoulders, continued on up the path that led to the top of the ridge. Yes, it was nice to be away from all the strictness of Miss Metcalfe's school—except for Susannah and Betsey. She missed her friends dreadfully, for what was the good of being able to run through the woods if there was no one to share it with?

Mattie's shoulders drooped. Once again the burdens of her young life settled themselves on her back. She had escaped from Miss Metcalfe—but to what? To the everyday world of cooking and cleaning and running a household so that her parents would be free to cut a new life out of a rocky hillside in the wilds of the New Hampshire Grants or, to use the French name, Vermont.

For five summers her father had packed his tools and journeyed from their house in western Massachusetts to the Grants, where, year after year, he attempted to carve out a farm. He had purchased the land from a stranger for a bag of flour and ten pieces of gold. The stranger had handed him the deed, wished him luck, and vanished, little knowing the havoc the deal had wreaked in the Hardwicke family.

Mattie had lain awake that night, listening to her parents as they argued. Her mother, Elizabeth, was furious that her husband had thrown away their hard-earned savings on a piece of land he had never even seen.

"But, Lizzie!" protested Mattie's father, "This is the opportunity of a lifetime. Just think—one hundred and forty-three acres of prime farmland in the middle of a new territory! You know I've always hankered for a place of my own, and this may be my only chance. All the good land around here is bought up. This is going to work, Lizzie, and then I'll build you that fine house you always wanted, I swear."

"Why can't you be content to be a blacksmith like your pa?" Mattie heard the bitterness in her mother's voice. Their voices died down to whispers, and Mattie fell asleep.

The promise of the fine house must have worked its magic, for in the morning Mattie awoke to find her mother busily preparing for her father's departure.

Mattie still remembered that day. She and her mother, her two young brothers, and her grandfather stood and waved as her father drove off with a heavily laden wagon and two horses. They had heard not a word of news of him until five months later, when he returned with one horse and no wagon. He was gaunt and tired, but his eyes sparkled as he described his Promised Land to his family.

The prime farmland was a "bit rocky," and the fine house was a lean-to shelter, but "oh, Lizzie, wait till you see the view!"

Mr. Hardwicke worked in the forge all winter like a madman, pounding out tools and horseshoes for fourteen hours a day to earn money for the family to live on while he was gone in the summer. Then in May, he packed his tools on his remaining horse and vanished again until early December. This routine went on for four years. Mattie and her mother never knew when or if he would return. But he conquered floods and droughts, hailstorms and wild critters, until he cleared enough land and built a real cabin.

Over the years Mattie grew up. She attended Miss Metcalfe's school and helped her mother at home, learning to cook and sew and do fancywork like all "fine young ladyes." Her grandfather kept the forge going in the summer and did a steady business. Although they all planned to move north someday, that day seemed far in the future.

Then, in December 1768, Mr. Hardwicke returned and announced, "Next year, we'll all go."

Mattie had mixed feelings. She looked forward to a new adventure, but her eagerness was tempered by the knowledge that she would be expected to take charge of the housekeeping. Her younger brothers were ecstatic, but in March they both became ill with a fever, and it was decided they would stay with Aunt Patience until the rest of the family returned in late fall. "The cabin is too isolated to stay in all winter," said Mr. Hardwicke.

"We'll come back here for the winter."

So, in early May 1769, four of them set out: Mattie, her parents, and her grandfather. The original plan was for Gramps to stay with Aunt Patience too, but a spell in the village stocks for public drunkenness changed that. Mattie's mother, embarrassed by her father-in-law, insisted he come along so she could keep her disapproving eye on him.

Mattie waved tearfully to her friends from the back of the wagon. She felt lonesome for the first time in her life. She didn't even have the company of her pesky brothers.

But soon there was no time for loneliness. The Hardwickes met up with other travelers, single men and families like them, who were journeying eagerly to the "Green Mountain" territory. Soon settled areas were left behind, and the smooth road gave way to a pitted and potholed surface. They followed the military road as far as they could, but even it, built ten years before, was little more than a track.

The journey turned into a haze for Mattie. They crossed and recrossed rivers, went up hills and down, and at one point the men had to unhitch the horses and pull the wagons themselves. The trip dragged on for days and then weeks as Mattie wearily plodded alongside the wagon. Her bones ached from sleeping on the ground, and not even the campfire at night could dispel the chill of the mountain air. One by one the families and men dropped out of the group as their destinations were reached, until only the Hardwickes remained. Finally, one late afternoon, just when Mattie felt she could go on no longer, her father called out, "There it is!"

Mattie looked up, expecting to see Heaven itself. She saw a tiny cabin squatting on a hillside. Beyond it, trees rose up to the top of a ridge. All around and below it was open meadow, with cornfields just visible to the left.

With a sudden spurt of energy she followed her father up the track to the cabin. It was made of logs, seamed with mud. A stone fireplace dominated one side. The cabin was windowless, and the doorway did not even have a door.

Mattie's mother sank to the ground beside her. "Oh, God help us! What have we gotten into?"

"But Lizzie, just look at that view!"

That had all been just three weeks ago. Those three weeks had been filled with activity. Mattie's parents had gone right to work in the fields, while Mattie had put the cabin to rights and set up her "kitchen." Gramps disappeared for hours at a time, never telling where he went. Slowly, life settled down and took on a routine, and now, for the first time in weeks, Mattie had a free moment.

Mattie sat and rested her back against a warm rock. Below her, a creek gurgled and she watched a hawk circling lazily in the sky. The sun and fresh air felt wonderful after the weeks in the windowless cabin, but Mattie was no longer accustomed to sitting still. Her restless legs demanded she get up, so she decided to explore a little.

She stood at the top of the ridge. Behind her lay the path back to the cabin, and before her lay a deep gorge. The sides were strewn with large boulders and out-croppings of rock, and far below, at the bottom, ran a small creek. Mattie scrambled down the boulders, picking her way carefully. She knew if she missed a step it could mean a nasty fall, and help was far away, over the ridge.

She finally reached the creek and, perching on a boulder, leaned over and dipped her hand into the water. Ouch! It was icy cold, and Mattie drew back. Perhaps later in the summer she could go wading, but certainly not today. Mattie sat back on her boulder and looked around. It really was a beautiful spot. The gorge was lined with a profusion of spring greenery, young plants clinging tenaciously to the rocks, springing out of clefts. Birds sang merrily in the trees at the top, and Mattie heard a woodpecker knocking.

Mattie looked up at the sky. The sun was lower—it was time to go back to start dinner. She reluctantly stood up and searched for the easiest route to the top. To her left, a series of boulders formed giant steps up the side. She crawled over to the bottom one and, looking down, noticed a hole to the side of it. A bush grew across the front of it, making the hole invisible except from the boulder. Mattie crouched down and peered in. It was a cave! She looked closer, but she could see little.

"I'll have to come back with a light," she thought. "How exciting to find my very own cave!"

The sun had sunk lower in the sky, so Mattie hurried

up the boulders and down the path to the cabin. To-morrow she had to do the washing, but afterward, she would come back to explore her cave.

The next morning Mattie rushed through her chores. She washed the breakfast dishes, then put a pot of water to boil over the fire. "Thank goodness I don't have to wash very often," she thought as she dragged out the heavy washtub.

By the time all the clothes were washed, her hands were raw and her arms and back ached. She gratefully hung the last shirt on the clothesline and dumped the washtub behind the cabin. She stretched back and forth to relieve the kinks in her back. Now she could go!

Mattie untied her apron and hung it on a nail near the door. She placed a small candle and a tinderbox in the pocket of her everyday calico dress. She felt a twinge of guilt. Candles were a precious commodity since they had brought only a dozen with them. Her father had said they would not need light in the evening as the days grew longer, and he was right—only one had been used so far. Perhaps no one would notice she had taken it.

Mattie strode to the ridge, her muscles complaining after the morning's heavy work. She ignored the discomfort, and as she got closer to the cave, she hurried even faster.

The cave was easy to find now. The morning sun came into the opening of the cave and made it much brighter than it had been the afternoon before. Mattie made a small pile of tinder and repeatedly struck her flint and steel together. She soon had a bright flame and carefully lit her candle from it.

It was still dark at the back of the cave, and she looked around eagerly as the light lit up the dark areas. The cave was the size of a small room, high enough to stand in. It was dry and had none of the mustiness Mattie expected. As she held the candle close to the wall, she saw faint pictures etched in the stone. She examined them closely.

Next to the entrance, there were two figures. They appeared to be girls, both dressed in tunics. The figures were smiling and were connected at the hands. Overhead was a crude figure of a bird, and around the second girl was a scattering of raindrop shapes. Next to the girls was tall flower with spiky petals. The next picture showed one girl lying down with spots instead of a face. The standing girl wore a frown. The next picture was even more of a puzzle. The prone figure had no

spots or face and the other girl was kneeling, the bird beside her. Finally, the last picture showed the first girl and the bird all surrounded by the raindrop shapes.

"What on earth can this be?" wondered Mattie aloud. "And who would have drawn these pictures?" As far as Mattie knew, the territory was wilderness, and they were the first to settle it, except for . . .

"Indians!" exclaimed Mattie. "An Indian must have carved these pictures!" She studied the last drawing again. "This girl is in all the drawings—I bet she's the one who carved them. But what happened to her friend? And what do the bird and the drops of water mean?"

As Mattie pondered this, her candlelight fell upon a small niche in the back wall. She hurried over to it and shined her light on it.

The niche formed a small shelf, and to Mattie's amazement, the shelf held a small clay pot. Mattie lifted the pot and carefully set it on the floor. It was round and had a tight-fitting lid.

"Indian gold!" she thought, breathless with excitement. "I'm rich!"

But Mattie's hopes plummeted as she saw the pot held nothing but dried corn. She ran her fingers through the kernels. "Now, why would someone go to all the trouble of putting corn in a cave?"

Disappointed, she replaced the pot on the shelf. The candle was burning down, so she snuffed it out and crawled out of the cave. All the way home she mulled over the puzzle of the drawings and the pot of corn.

At dinner that evening, Mattie asked her father, "Are there any Indians here?"

Gramps jerked upright, then hastily resumed eating, as if trying to cover up his surprise. Mattie's mother gave him a stern look, and she said, "I certainly hope not!"

Her father replied, "Actually, there very well may be, although the officials all deny it. In fact, if I hadn't been able to trade an old Indian for a sack of corn that first year, I might not have survived at all."

"You never told me that," said Mattie's mother.

"I didn't want to worry you. Besides, they were very peaceful."

"Peaceful! They're savages! They sided with the French in the war, remember?"

"Now, Lizzie, you just get down off your high horse," interjected Gramps. "There ain't no Injuns here now."

She gave the old man a withering look. "How do you know?"

He looked startled and flustered. "I just know, that's all," he said, and Mattie tried to change the subject.

"Where did the Indian get the corn, Pa?" she asked.

"He grew it," he replied. "The Indians grew all kinds of things, like corn and beans and squash. They gathered a lot of wild plants too. Tell you what—tomorrow we'll go exploring and see if we can find any edibles."

Mattie agreed and rose to help her mother with the dishes. As she dried, she thought again about the Indians and the pot of corn.

The next day was Sunday. Back home in Massachusetts, they would all have gone to church, but that was
impossible now. After breakfast, Pa got out the Bible
and read aloud for a while. Then Gramps said a prayer,
mostly about blessings and Providence and deliverance
and such, then their worship was over for the week.

Since it was Sunday, Mattie's mother wouldn't let
them work in the fields, even though they were eager to
get their corn planted. Instead, they all set out for a walk
through the woods. Mattie carried a basket in case they
found anything worth gathering.

Her father pointed out many edible greens. Even the
young ferns were tasty, and soon Mattie had a basketful.
Her father had learned a great deal about surviving in
the forest from a fur trapper he met up with that first
year.

"Funny fellow," said Pa. "He was part French and
part Indian, but he spoke English too. Knew everything
there was to know about this country. Right smart
fellow, but he said he couldn't stay in one place long. He
stayed with me about a week, but one morning he was
gone, just like that." He didn't add that the trapper had
taken one of his horses, leaving behind a bundle of furs
and some tobacco. Pa considered the wealth of infor-
mation he had acquired from the man to be well worth
the loss of his horse.

The rest of the day was spent at the cabin. Gramps sat
in the sun and whittled, while Pa mended the harness
and groomed the horses, jobs he was too tired to

undertake during the week. Mattie's mother was content to sit and mend clothes and darn socks while Mattie planted flower seeds outside the cabin.

Mattie's mother paused in her mending and smiled. "The place might even look like home once those flowers come up." Mattie nodded, but she knew that they would be a far cry from the formal garden her mother had always dreamed of.

"I saw some right pretty wildflowers in the woods," spoke up Gramps. "There's some interesting plants up here in the wilderness."

Mattie's mother looked at him sharply. "Since when did you get interested in plants?"

"I'll have you know, young lady, that I used to be quite a woodsman. I traveled all over Massachusetts and lived off the land. That is, until I married my Martha. But even then, in the early years, she and I would go off in the spring and spend a few weeks in the woods. Of course, that was before the place got overrun with people. Yes, those were good times." He lapsed back into silence.

Mrs. Hardwicke's face softened. "I guess you still miss her, don't you?" she said, but the old man did not reply.

Mattie smoothed the soft earth over the seeds and sat back on her heels. Her father walked over from the shelter they laughingly referred to as "the Barn."

"How about helping us plant corn tomorrow, Mattie?" he called.

"Sure," said Mattie.

"I'll even do the housework tomorrow for a change," added her mother.

Mattie smiled agreement. "Can I have my own patch of corn?" she asked.

"Certainly," said her father. "I have just the spot. It's near the cabin and should be fine ground for your crop."

The next morning Mattie gladly left the dishes to her mother and followed her father to the field. She hoisted the sack of corn seed over her shoulder and was soon working in a steady rhythm. One, two, three, four, space, one, two, three, four, space. At the end of one row, her back started to kink. One, two, three, four, space. After an hour, her backbone screamed in agony as she straightened up.

"Take a break and walk around a bit," suggested her father.

Mattie nodded and thankfully dropped the sack of corn to the ground. She walked into the woods and wandered up the path to the ridge. Almost without realizing it, she found herself at the entrance to the cave.

She had no candle with her this time, but she crawled in and instinct led her straight back to the niche. She groped for the clay pot and carried it outside. She sat on the boulder and looked at the corn in the sunlight.

"This corn must have been special to the girl in the pictures," she thought. "I don't suppose it's stealing if I take some of it to plant."

She took off her apron and scooped out half of the

seeds and laid them in the center. She carried the pot
back to its niche and replaced it. Then she crawled out
and gathered up the edges of her apron into a bundle.

"No sense in letting it go to waste," she said as she
turned and climbed up the rocks toward home.

By midafternoon Mattie was almost finished planting
the Indian corn. Her father had given her the promised

plot of ground, and it was just the right size for her to tend by herself.

She was halfway down the last row when she heard someone calling in the distance. She looked up to see a man on a horse riding up the straggling path to the cabin. He waved his hat and yelled.

Mattie's father stood up warily. He glanced over at his shotgun, leaning against a stump. But as the rider got closer, he relaxed and strode off to greet him.

"Harry Miller!" he called out. The two men shook hands enthusiastically. "You old dog—what brings you out here? You're looking well."

"So're you, Hardwicke," replied Mr. Miller. "I come to tell you the news."

"News? What news?"

"We've got us a town," said Mr. Miller. "They got word yesterday."

"A town. How about that! Come on to the cabin." He turned to Mattie and waved. "Come here, Mattie. I want you to meet a friend of mine." Mattie joined the men and her father said, "Mattie, this is Harry Miller. My daughter Martha, Harry."

Mattie bobbed a little curtsy, her head ducked down, just as Miss Metcalfe had taught her was proper when meeting a gentleman. Not that Mr. Miller was a real gentleman, but it paid to stay in practice.

"Well, bless me," he said. "I ain't been curtsied to in ages."

The three walked to the cabin, where Mattie's mother was preparing dinner.

"Lizzie," Mr. Hardwicke called out. "Look who's here. This is Harry Miller. He's the one who helped me with the fireplace. This is my wife, Elizabeth."

"Pleased to know you, Mistress Hardwicke." Harry Miller gave her a stately bow. He turned to Mr. Hardwicke. "Looks like the chimney's holding up well."

"Aye, that it is. Sure beats a hole in the ceiling. Lizzie, where's Gramps? I want him to meet Harry."

"Oh, he's off goodness knows where."

"Ah, no matter. Come and sit down, Harry, and tell us about the town."

"Town?" echoed Mrs. Hardwicke.

"That's right," said Mr. Miller. "'Course, you know where Olly Harper put up his trading post. Well, some fellow by the name of Gardner come and put up a grist mill just upstream, and now folks have been moving in from all over. There's talk of sending for a preacher, even. I never would have believed it. Sure won't be the same."

"What'd they name it?" asked Mattie's father.

"Well, there was some as wanted to name it Kingston, but we settled on Gardner's Mills, seeing as how John Gardner will probably do more for us than old King George ever would."

The two men fell into a discussion of politics, and Mattie and her mother looked at each other, each reading the other's thoughts. A town meant stores and churches and schools and other families. But best of all, a town meant new friends.

Gramps did not take kindly to the idea of a new town springing up.

"Oh, Lordy," he groaned. "Now the place will be ruined for sure."

"Nonsense!" snapped Mattie's mother. "A town will be good for all of us. And don't blaspheme."

"Now, you listen to me, young lady," sputtered Gramps. "I'm not blaspheming, and people will destroy this place. Before you know it, there won't be a tree left in the whole territory. The people will be crawling all over the place, just like back home."

"Why shouldn't more people come here? There's enough land for thousands of people. Why shouldn't they have the same opportunity as we had to make a new life?" Mattie's mother threw down her dishcloth. "I for one am glad there'll be people here."

The battle raged until Mattie's father stepped in. "Lizzie's got a point, Pa. We came here and built our farm, but that doesn't give us the right to say no one else can. This is a tough way to live, and I don't imagine there's too many more people as crazy as us to want to do it. These mountains will take care of themselves."

Gramps stomped out of the cabin, and Mattie sighed. Gramps hadn't always been so cantankerous. She remembered when she was a little girl and had spent hours at a time in the forge, watching her father and Gramps as they worked their magic, shaping and bending the hard metal. They had been happy then. But when her grandmother died, Gramps had changed. He had grown sullen and bitter and fought constantly with his daughter-in-law. He began spending hours in the taverns and finally ended up in disgrace, sentenced to a day in the stocks on the village common, jeered at by the townspeople.

But since coming to the Vermont territory, he seemed better. Perhaps the absence of the spirits he had previously used to drown his sorrows had improved his disposition. But Mattie suspected it was the hours that he spent away from the cabin. Perhaps he had found peace in those woods, just as she had found peace and tranquility in the little Indian cave by the water.

It was two weeks before the Hardwickes could go to town. Mattie and her mother were all for hitching up the horses immediately, but her father insisted on finishing the planting. Then one of the horses went lame and the weather turned to rain. But soon the sky cleared and the horses were fit, and they were ready to go.

Mattie put on her best dress. Made by her mother, it was of a lightly woven dark blue muslin with a little white collar that Mattie had embroidered herself. The sleeves were slightly puffed, the cuffs tight. Mattie twirled around, then dropped a sweeping curtsy to her mother.

"Good thing I made that dress too big last winter," said her mother. "It just fits now. My, how you've grown! Soon you'll be putting up your hair and looking for a beau."

Mattie blushed. She felt her father looking at her searchingly.

"Why, I do declare you're right, Lizzie. I hadn't realized my little girl had grown so much. But don't go rushing off to get married yet, Mattie." He chucked her under the chin. "You've got a cornfield to tend."

The newly named village of Gardner's Mills perched on the side of a small river that boiled down from the high mountains. A natural road ran alongside the banks. First a path for animals, then a road for the Indians of the region, it had been widened and smoothed by the new settlers into a heavily traveled thoroughfare.

The village had begun as a trading post built by a fur trader. As the number of settlers increased over the years, the trading post had prospered and expanded from a birchbark hut to a real wooden building.

In 1768, John Gardner had been drawn to the area to build his grist mill. It was a natural spot for a mill, the river banks high enough not to flood in the spring and just the right height for the big water wheel that turned the millstones. Even the river could be relied on to flow swiftly enough all summer long. Only the very frigid temperatures of deep winter could stop the river, freezing it even as it tumbled downward, forming a beautiful winter scene.

There was little enough of the village when Mattie first saw it that Sunday of June 1769. Besides the trading post—now a general store—and the mill, there were only a few crude cabins and sheds. There was evidence of building, though, as men hurried here and there and wagons clattered past on the road.

Mr. Hardwicke pulled up in front of the store, and Mattie climbed down stiffly. The five-mile trip had taken over an hour, but Mattie was buoyed by excitement. Gardner's Mills was not much of a town, but after months of isolation, it was a sight for sore eyes.

Mr. Hardwicke tied the horses to a post. "Let's go on over to the store, and I'll introduce you to Olly," he said.

As Mattie stepped into the low, dark building, she took a deep breath. The smell of tobacco, sawdust, and dried apples enveloped her, and she looked around eagerly. Goods of every description lined the walls. There was everything a settler might need: bags of flour and cornmeal, lumpy sacks of potatoes, tin cookware, candles, leather harness, even a small selection of leather-bound books. A small man with a long beard hopped around the store, calling out prices and dickering rapidly with a customer as he piled up provisions. He caught sight of the Hardwickes and, without pausing, said, "Well, Hardwicke, thought maybe you was dead." He turned back to his customer. "I'm out of lard, but I'll have some in a fortnight. Salt's in short supply, so a pound will have to do you." The clink of coins signaled the close of the transaction, and as the customer left, the little man turned back to Mattie's father.

"So I see you brought the wife and kids with you. Doing well, are you? Well, I'm glad you stopped in

today, I might not be here next week. I've done sold out
to my cousin," he said in response to Mr. Hardwicke's
raised eyebrows. Olly Harper fussed around the store,
talking nonstop, barely pausing for breath.

"That's what comes of living alone in the woods for so
long," whispered Mr. Hardwicke to Mattie. "Got used
to the sound of his own voice."

The Hardwickes walked around the store, choosing
their purchases to the background of Olly Harper's
patter. Mr. Hardwicke bought a new sharpening stone.
Mrs. Hardwicke needed flour, salt, and a paper of
needles. She pressed a coin into Mattie's hand.

"That's yours to spend as you like."

Mattie looked around. The penny candy looked
tempting. There was a tiny ladies' looking glass that
caught her eye, but she didn't have enough money for
such a luxury. Then she saw what she wanted on a
dusty shelf in the back—a small bottle of ink and a
dozen sheets of writing paper.

The Hardwickes completed their purchases and
escaped from the garrulous little man, wishing him luck
in his new venture.

"Goodness," said Mrs. Hardwicke as they stepped
outside. Mr. Hardwicke grinned. "Olly sure is something, isn't he? I'm not surprised he's moving on. He's a
fur trader, not a merchant. There's some that don't take
kindly to his Indian wife, either. Still, if it wasn't for him,
there wouldn't be a town here."

Mr. Hardwicke went off to the new mill while Mattie
and her mother took their picnic lunch down to a shady

spot near the river. They laid out the food and rested, drinking in the loveliness of the countryside.

Soon Mr. Hardwicke returned, almost running in his excitement. "Guess what, Lizzie!" He pulled his wife to her feet. "John Gardner just hired me for the winter as a blacksmith!"

Mrs. Hardwicke stammered, "Wh-wh-what? Hired as a blacksmith? But I thought you wanted to be a farmer!"

"It's only for the winter. He's building the smithy now, with a cabin to go with it. We can move into town for the winter while I work. With the money I'll earn, we can hire a man to work on the farm. Come spring, we can send for the boys."

"We won't have to make that long trip back home to Massachusetts," breathed Mrs. Hardwicke. "I have to admit I was dreading that trip."

The two fell to making plans while Mattie silently ate her lunch. Not going back to Massachusetts! She wouldn't be seeing her friends again after all. Once again, loneliness engulfed her as she surveyed the tiny town. As a prospective winter residence, it left a lot to be desired. Mattie sighed. There were several months before winter set in. Perhaps a miracle would happen and someone her own age would come to town. Surely one of these days she would find a friend, even in the wilds of the Green Mountains.

Mattie's corn grew taller and taller as the summer deepened. She and her family spent most of that summer gathering and growing food and preparing it for storage. Berries were picked and dried or made into jelly. Wild greens were eaten fresh or taken into town and sold. Mr. Hardwicke fished and hunted, and any extra meat was dried or smoked in the big chimney. Onions were tied into bunches and hung from the rafters. The root crops stayed in the ground and would be dug up right before the move to town.

Mattie often went to the small creek and visited the cave. She waded in the chilly water and watched as the days shortened and the once-green gorge faded into red and gold and orange.

The time came for harvest, and the whole family worked relentlessly. First they picked the corn, then husked it, then poured the dried kernels into sacks.

Mattie kept her corn separate from the main crop. It was a little coarser and darker, and her father said it was only fit for feed corn, but she didn't care. She filled three sacks with her harvest, all from just a few handfuls of seed.

The days grew shorter and colder, and soon the ground itself began to freeze. The cabin was made snug with more mud in the cracks, and Mr. Hardwicke made a door for the opening. Firewood was cut and stacked neatly, ready for the family when they came back in the spring. All the food was transported into town, and the time came for the family to move too.

The day before they left, Mattie returned to the cave. The gorge was now bare of green, and dry leaves crunched underfoot. The wind whistled through the cut, and Mattie hugged her shawl closer, clutching the small bundle she carried.

Inside the cave, she lifted down the clay pot. She poured in seeds from her harvest, filling the pot back up to the top. Then she added a sheet of paper. She had written a short note for the next visitor, telling her name and the date and how she had grown the corn.

"I wonder if anyone will ever find this cave," she thought. "And will I ever have a friend to bring here, to share this wonderful secret with?"

They were loading the last of the dishes and clothes onto the wagon when Gramps suddenly appeared out of the woods. He was dressed in a buckskin coat and carried his gun.

"Well, finally!" exclaimed Mattie's mother. "It's about time you showed up. Off on one of your wanderings again, I see. Well, we'll put a stop to that when we move to town. Folks'll think you're wandering in your wits, going off for weeks at a time. Bah!"

"I'm not going to town," he said in a quiet voice.

"What?" exclaimed Mr. Hardwicke. "You can't stay here by yourself. You'd freeze!"

"I'm not staying. I'm going north." He took a deep breath. "You may as well know, I've joined up with an Indian tribe that's been living near here. It's time for them to move on, and I'm going too."

Mattie looked with surprise at her grandfather. He grinned a little, and suddenly the years of care that had

been etched in his face evaporated. She saw a young man, gray-bearded perhaps, but a young man nonetheless, with a twinkle in his eye.

"Indians?" said Mattie in surprise. "I thought you said there weren't any Indians around here."

"Well, I lied, punkin. They used to stay the summer way down on the river, but the white man's pushed them up this creek. They're real cautious 'bout being seen."

Mattie's mother flapped her jaw, speechless.

Her father said, "So that's where you've been, you old devil. I wondered what was drawing you to the woods. I figured you had a still hidden away."

Gramps laughed. "No, no still. Better—a new wife."

Mrs. Hardwicke sputtered, then finally found her voice. "A-a-a wife? An Indian woman?"

"Yes, a fine woman, and one that doesn't nag." He glared meaningfully at his daughter-in-law. Mattie could hardly stifle her laughter. Gramps, the old Gramps, was back, but she would be losing him again so soon.

She ran to her grandfather and hugged him. "Oh, Gramps, I'll miss you."

"I'll miss you, too, lassie. But we'll be back through in the spring. Don't worry—you'll see me again, I promise." The old man shook hands with his son, and they embraced. Then he picked up his gun and a small bag of his belongings and turned away.

"Stop him!" shrieked Mrs. Hardwicke. "Go after him—he can't do this!"

"Nay, Lizzie," said Mattie's father. "He'll be fine. He's chosen his way."

Mattie ran after her grandfather and called out, "Gramps, what's your Indian name?"

He turned and smiled. "Ironbeard," he called. "My name is Ironbeard." Then he vanished into the woods.

"Good-bye, Ironbeard," whispered Mattie. "Good-bye and good luck."

Mattie hardly recognized the town of Gardner's Mills. It had mushroomed seemingly overnight. The store was enlarged and flanked by a new house, with lace curtains at the real glass windows. The mill had expanded into a maze of warehouses, and everywhere new cabins had sprung up. Trees had been cut down, and only the river looked the same—but even that was now spanned by a footbridge.

Mattie's father pulled up behind a newly built cabin across the wide road from the store. It was smaller than the cabin on the farm, but it was snugly built, with a real glass window and a fireplace that bore the stamp of Harry Miller's craftsmanship. Next door stood the smithy, a large chimney protruding up through the center of the building, with a stable for horses to one side, connected by a paddock. Behind the cabin stood a tiny chicken coop and a door that led down to the root cellar, now stocked full of winter vegetables.

Mattie jumped down from the wagon and went into the cabin. Their beds were already set up, with fluffy feather ticks and warm quilts. Next to the fireplace on the right was a work table and several shelves for storage. A plank table with benches stood in the middle of the room, covered with a homespun tablecloth and adorned with some late fall flowers. All in all, the cabin was cozy, and Mattie saw from her mother's expression that she too was pleased.

The two unloaded the wagon, and soon the cabin really did look like home, with their dishes on the shelves, long dresses on pegs on the wall, and even a framed sampler on the wall.

Mr. Hardwicke came in and nodded. "Looks fine, Lizzie. We'll be snug as bugs this winter. Mattie, why don't we take your corn to the mill and get it ground? Now, before I unhitch the horses."

They drove the wagon over to the mill, and Mr. Hardwicke hoisted a bag of corn on his shoulder. Mattie followed him into the building.

She was struck by the noise as she walked inside. Water rushed by outside, turning the big wheel, which in turn powered the huge millstones that ground the corn into powder. Sacks of grain stood everywhere, and a fine dust fogged the air.

"Hello, Tom," Mattie's father called out to a young man. As Mattie watched, he picked up a sack of grain and tossed it to one side effortlessly. He was tall and powerfully built, with sandy hair that framed a strong jaw. As he approached the Hardwickes, Mattie saw that his eyes were a deep blue, and although she had thought him to be much older, from his unlined face she guessed him to be only a few years older than herself.

She bobbed a short curtsy to him as her father introduced them. As Tom Gardner smiled and bowed slightly, her heart unexpectedly turned over, and suddenly she felt very awkward.

Tom bent and opened the sack of corn.

"This is Indian corn," he said, raising his voice against the roar of machinery. "Where'd you get it?"

Mattie opened her mouth to reply, but just then a man stuck his head through the door and called to Tom. He excused himself and hurried away, and her father moved the sack to a pile near the door.

"We'll leave them here and pick them up later," he said. "This is a busy time for the mill."

Mattie's shoulders drooped. "Tom probably thinks I'm just a little girl with nothing to say for myself," she thought.

After her father had taken the remaining sacks into the mill, Mattie climbed onto the wagon seat. As Mr. Hardwicke picked up the reins, she saw Tom hurrying toward them. She smiled as he called to her.

"I'll have your corn for you tomorrow if you'd like to come for it then," he said. "It was nice to meet you," he called out as the wagon pulled away.

Mattie turned and waved. She couldn't wait for tomorrow to come!

As Mattie opened the door to the cabin, she heard voices. A woman and a young girl were seated at the table drinking tea with her mother.

"Oh, here's Mattie now," said her mother. "Mattie, I'd like you to meet Mrs. Harper and her daughter Pauline."

Mattie curtsied and hung up her cloak. She sat down to a cup of tea, and as her mother and Mrs. Harper prattled on, she studied the other girl. Pauline had smooth yellow hair that hung in two braids, china blue eyes, and a pixie face. She smiled at Mattie hesitantly, and Mattie grinned back.

"How old are you?" Mattie asked.

"I'm eleven. And you?"

"Thirteen in December. How long have you been in Gardner's Mills?"

"We came in August. My pa bought the store from his cousin. Are you really going to be staying? I've been so lonesome."

"At least for the winter. But our farm is only five miles away. You can come and visit anytime. And I know what you mean about being lonesome. I'm so glad to meet another girl after all these months."

Mrs. Harper stood up and said, "Well, Elizabeth, I'm so glad to have made your acquaintance. It's so fortunate that the town is attracting quality folk, if you know what I mean. Come along, Pauline dear. Please stop in anytime," she said as she shook hands with Mrs. Hardwicke.

"Good-bye, Pauline," said Mattie.

"My friends call me Polly," she replied, "and I know we're going to be good friends."

"Yes, I'm sure we are," said Mattie.

She closed the door and went to the window to watch the retreating figures of the Harpers as they hurried into their house across the road. A gentle snow had begun to fall, covering the town with a blanket of white down.

Mattie looked out at the little town. It wasn't much, but across the road was a new friend, and down at the mill Tom Gardner himself was grinding her corn, her Indian corn.

Her mother came to the window. "Well, it looks like Gardner's Mills might not be such a bad place to live after all."

"I agree," said Mattie. "I think it's going to be a special place for a long, long time to come."

The snow drifted down, covering the mountains, the trees, the farms. It fell on the creek, frosting the boulders and gently sifting into the opening of the little cave. Snug on its shelf, the little pot of Indian corn stood, wrapped in the silence of winter, just waiting for spring and another chance at new life.

Stacy

— ❖ —

"Where do you want your dresser, honey?"

Stacy looked up from the packing case where she sat. Her mother stood in the doorway, hair in a scarf, dirt streaked on one cheek. Behind her, the two men from the moving company patiently held an antique-white dresser.

"Oh, I don't know. I guess over there." Stacy gestured to the wall by the window. "It doesn't matter," she thought. "This will never look like my room."

Stacy watched the burly men ease the chest into position without a word. Her mom smiled at her and left, chattering to the men about where she wanted the piano. Stacy listlessly picked up an old towel and dusted off the dresser.

"What a dump!" she said, throwing the towel on the floor. She flopped down onto the unmade bed and glumly surveyed the room, listing its faults. "The wallpaper's torn, the paint is peeling everywhere, and there's not even a stinking carpet on the floor."

She tilted her head. "It's not even level, for heaven's sake," she complained.

Stacy thought back to that awful day two months before, when her father announced that he had gotten a new job in Vermont. Stacy's life had been shattered, but her parents were ecstatic.

"No more traffic, no smog, no noisy neighbors!" they sang.

"I'm going to die," thought Stacy.

"Fresh air, clean water, the beauty of the mountains. Aren't you excited, Stace?"

"No, I'm not. I don't want to move. New Jersey's my home. I like it here."

"Don't worry about her," they had said when she stormed off to her room. "She'll get used to it. She just needs time."

But she hadn't gotten used to it. She had hated Vermont at first sight, and she especially disliked this "antique farmhouse." She longed for the haven of her old room, with its deep wall-to-wall carpeting and the central air conditioner gently hissing out cool air. She had had her own phone, too, with dozens of friends at the other end of the line. Dozens.

Stacy's throat tightened. No, she wouldn't cry. Not here, not in this place.

She jumped to her feet and ran out of the room, down the bare wooden stairs and through the maze of rooms on the ground floor. She found the back door and pushed through.

The back yard was a mass of weeds, disguising mounds of forgotten farm equipment. She threaded her way through the jungle of piled-up boards and heaps of rocks. When she reached the cool canopy of trees at the edge of the clearing, she didn't stop but plunged deeper into the woods. A path rose steeply before her as she stumbled on, weaving in and out of trees, over massive boulders, brushing past unfamiliar bushes and undergrowth. At the top of a ridge, she paused, panting from her climb, the unshed tears burning her eyes. She collapsed onto a moss-covered rock.

Misery overwhelmed her as the first tears fell. "I hate this place. Why can't I go home? It's not fair, it's just not fair," she sobbed. "The whole gang is having fun without me. I wonder if anyone misses me? They're probably all out at the mall," she thought, then changed her mind. "No, it's getting hot, so they're at the pool." She tormented herself with visions of her old gang until she could cry no more.

The moss under her hand tickled, and she looked up, suddenly aware of her surroundings. She had never been in a real forest before. Her sniffles died away as she sat very still and listened and looked, drinking in the new experience.

It seemed very quiet at first, but soon she was able to distinguish sounds. There was a bird somewhere off to her left, and an insect buzzed over her head. She heard water flowing over on the other side of the ridge, and she rose to investigate.

The ridge fell away sharply in a jumble of boulders. The stream was just visible far below, and Stacy gingerly climbed down. She was almost down to the water when the rock she had stepped on slipped and down she slid. She grabbed wildly at a stick to break her fall and shakily pulled herself up onto a boulder. Her ankle had been bruised in the fall, and she rubbed it as she looked around.

Her boulder jutted out over the stream. The stream itself was fairly wide, and the water flowed rapidly over the rocks that formed its bed. Here and there Stacy could see deep pools, and below her boulder was a small backwash. She turned and looked at the side of the gorge she had just descended.

"Wow," she thought. "It sure looks steeper from this angle." She began to consider how she would get back up. She stood and surveyed the area.

To her left a group of boulders formed a series of steps leading upward. She scrambled over to the first one and looked for a foothold. Then she looked more closely. Hidden behind a large bush was an opening in the rocks. She crept closer and peered into the opening.

"Neat," she said. "A cave! A real cave!"

The opening was about two and a half feet across, and Stacy was just about to crawl in when she thought, "What if there's a bear or something in there?" She looked and listened intently, then picked up a small

rock and threw it into the opening. No angry bear charged out, so she slowly stuck her head into the cave.

The cave was pitch black. The light from outside only penetrated a few feet, and she could make out only the rock walls. It didn't appear to be more than about six feet wide.

Stacy withdrew her head and backed away. "A flashlight," she thought. "I better get a flashlight."

She studied the position of the cave so she could find

it again when she returned. It was only visible from the bottom boulder of the rock steps. As Stacy climbed up the boulders, she memorized her route. At the top of the ridge, she paused to get her bearings, then ran headlong down the rough path to the farmhouse. The misery that had driven her into the woods was completely forgotten.

By the time Stacy got back to the house, the movers had gone. Her mother was sitting in the kitchen, her feet on a box, a can of soda in her hand. Stacy had never seen her usually neat mother so disheveled.

"Do we have a flashlight?" she asked.

Her mother looked blank. "A flashlight? What do you need a flashlight for?"

"Oh, I just wanted to do a little exploring," answered Stacy.

"Are you kidding? Exploring? Stace, we're in the middle of moving!" protested her mother. At Stacy's crestfallen look, however, she relented. "Okay, you can go exploring, but you have to unpack this box for me. And don't look like that—it's the one with the flashlight in it."

The box was full of silverware and kitchen utensils, which Stacy hastily placed in a drawer. At the bottom was the precious flashlight. She flashed it on and off to make sure it worked and headed for the door. Her mother called after her.

"Be careful, hon. The woods are dangerous. Are you sure you know what poison ivy looks like?"

"Don't worry, Mom. I'll be fine. I'm not going far." Stacy escaped out the door before her mother could delay her any longer.

She pointed the flashlight into the mouth of the cave. As the beams illuminated the interior, she pressed in closer. She flashed the light all around the cave and squeezed in. The cave was the size of a small room, about six feet wide at the opening, expanding to about fifteen feet at the back. It was dry and the air felt cool on her face. She found that she could stand comfortably, and she slowly let the light play over the stone walls. The floor was rock, with a scattering of sand that had blown into the opening over the years. There was no sign that the cave had ever been used, not even by wild animals.

"This will make a great hideout," thought Stacy. "I could bring down some pillows, maybe my radio. I wonder why the animals haven't used it? There's probably never been anyone near here. Just think—my first day in Vermont, and I've already discovered a cave!"

Stacy walked along the walls, letting the light probe all the cracks. The walls were rough, formed aeons ago by rock falling on rock. As Stacy neared the far wall, she spied a little niche in the wall. She flashed her light in it, and to her amazement, she saw a clay pot sitting on a rock ledge.

"Wow!" she exclaimed. "I guess I'm not the first to find this place after all!" She tucked the flashlight into the crook of her neck and slowly lowered the clay pot to the floor.

Stacy examined the pot closely. It was round, about eight inches in diameter, and it was etched with a cross-hatch design. It had a flat lid with no handle. Stacy grasped the edges and lifted the lid. She shined the light inside.

The pot was filled with dried corn kernels, and a piece of paper lay on top. As Stacy lifted the paper out of the pot, she felt the brittleness of very old parchment.

Gingerly, she unfolded the crackling paper and shining her light on the wispy handwriting, she began to read.

"'I found thif bowell in thif cave.' The s's all look like f's," said Stacy. "'It muft have been leff by a Indun girl. There waf corn in it and I planted it. I grewe more corn that I have plafed infide thif bowell. It if goode corn. I am twelfe yerf old and I wifhe I had a friend like the Indun girl drew bye the door. Maybee fomeone will reade thif letter fome day. Martha Anne Hardwicke, Mattie, Novembor 17, 1769.'"

Stacy couldn't believe it. 1769! "This is over two hundred years old!" she exclaimed. She reread the letter, deciphering the strange letters and misspelled words.

Stacy sat back on her heels. "Whew!" she breathed as the contents of the writing sunk in. "This pot has been sitting here for over two centuries just waiting for someone to come along and find it. Amazing."

Stacy turned the light back onto the walls of the cave.

There should be some kind of drawing, according to Mattie's note. Yes, there by the opening, a vague design was etched into the stone. It appeared to be stick figures with big smiles, and they were joined at the arms. "Maybe that showed they were friends," thought Stacy. She looked closely, and about three feet away were more etchings. One stick figure was standing up with a frown on her face. The other was lying down. "She looks sick," thought Stacy. "What can that mean?"

She continued on around the cave and found another picture of the two figures, then a final picture of just one figure and a bird, all encircled by water drops.

"Weird city," she thought. "There were two girls, and then I guess one got sick or something, because the last picture just shows the one girl."

She knelt at the bowl of corn, running her fingers through the kernels. "I wonder if the girl who did the drawings is the same one who put this pot here. And who was Mattie?"

The questions whirled through Stacy's head as she replaced the pot on the ledge and started home. Her homesickness vanished as she pondered the mysteries of her new cave.

Stacy was standing in the cave. It glowed with an eerie light and out of the shadows emerged people—old friends glimmered around her as an Indian girl stepped forward and took her hand. "Please be my friend," she whispered. Then the whisperings were replaced by another sound. A whirring filled the air—whirr, whirr . . .

Stacy awoke with a start. The whirring was coming from inside her room! In the darkness she felt, more than saw, a presence come swooping toward her. She screamed and dove under the covers as the monster swooped again.

The room light flipped on. "What's wr—oh my God, it's a bat!" Stacy heard her mother go flying down the hall, and she shuddered underneath the blankets.

"I'll get him! I'll get him!" Stacy heard her father shout. She peeped out over the top of the covers to see him dressed in his boxer shorts and his old fishing hat, brandishing a golf club. She started to laugh at the ludicrous sight, but just then the bat fluttered at her again, and she scrambled under the blankets once more.

Stacy lay rigid as her parents chased the bat around the room. Finally, after an eternity punctuated with "oohs" and "ahs" and "take that, you bat" and a few curses, the creature was persuaded to leave through the window. Stacy surfaced from under the blankets and saw her parents collapsed on the floor, panting.

"Whew!" said her father. "I wonder where he came from?"

"Probably the attic," said her mother.

Stacy sat bolt upright in bed. "How do you expect me to sleep in a room swarming with bats? How could you do this to me? That thing could have bit me!"

"It's okay, Stace," her father said as he picked up his golf club. "He was more scared of you than you were of him. Don't worry, we'll get rid of the bats."

"That's what you used to say about spiders," Stacy

retorted. She quickly jumped out of bed and switched on all the lights. Grabbing her old tennis racket, she settled into bed, determined to keep watch all night. But soon weariness conquered fear, and she dozed off once more.

Stacy awoke to the full glory of a summer's morning. The sun poured in the uncurtained window as she stretched, rubbing the kinks out of her neck. She looked around and shivered as she remembered the scare of the night before.

Her mother sat at the kitchen table, thumbing through a wallpaper sample book.

"Good morning, Stace." She smiled. "I was just looking over the samples for your room. What do you think will look good? Flowers? Hearts? Stripes, maybe?"

"I really don't care what you put in that room because I won't be here to see it. I'm going back to New Jersey," she announced.

"Stacy Ann, I don't like that tone of voice. And you are not going back to New Jersey. Where would you live?"

"But I hate it here! There's nothing to do, and I don't have any friends." Stacy collapsed onto a chair. "You just don't understand."

"Oh, honey, of course I understand. I miss my friends too. It's just going to take time. We just got here, and you can't expect everything to be the same as New Jersey. Give it a chance, okay?" Stacy stared glumly into her cereal bowl. "Look—after breakfast I have to go into town to see about getting someone to get rid of those bats. We'll pick out your new wallpaper, then we'll stop by the library. Maybe they have a summer program or something where you can meet some kids. Okay?"

"Okay," Stacy agreed reluctantly. "But I still don't like it here."

Stacy looked up at the frame two-story building. "This is the library? It's nothing but a dinky house." She had been expecting a sleek glass and chrome building like the public library in her old neighborhood. "I bet the most recent book is Winnie the Pooh," she grumbled.

"Oh, come on—and quit complaining," said her mother.

They stepped into the coolness of the building, and immediately Stacy wrinkled up her nose. "I knew it would smell," she said under her breath as her mother shot her a warning look.

A dark-haired woman stepped out of a door to the right. "Good morning," she said pleasantly.

"Good morning," said Stacy's mother. "We're new in town. I'm Karen Adams, and this is Stacy. We'd like to join the library."

"Wonderful! I'm Kathy Gardner. You must be the ones that bought the old Brooks place."

"Yes, we just finished moving in yesterday."

"Well, here, you can fill out these cards. My daughter is around here somewhere," she said to Stacy. "Oh, Jill!" she called out.

A girl popped through the doorway behind Stacy. "Yup, what is it?"

"I'd like you to meet someone. This is Mrs. Adams and her daughter—Stacy, wasn't it?" she said, hesitating.

"Yeah, Stacy," she replied as she and Jill gave each other the once-over. Jill was about Stacy's height, with short dark hair and glasses. She was dressed in standard uniform: scruffy jeans, dirty sneakers, and an oversize

t-shirt. Stacy looked down at her own outfit. They could almost be twins.

"Hi," said Jill. "Where'd you come from?"

"New Jersey," said Stacy.

"They bought the Brooks place," said Mrs. Gardner.

"Oh, good," Jill brightened. "That's just down the road from us. Come on, I'll show you around." She led Stacy out the door as their mothers resumed their conversation.

The library was actually a large house, with a central hall where the desk stood and rooms leading off to either side. Jill showed Stacy the adult section and the reference area, then led her into the children's room.

"Mom set up a new young adult section over here," she said. "What grade are you in?"

"I'll be in junior high, eighth grade."

"Me too. We go to River Valley. We can ride the bus together."

Stacy smiled. "Well, I'll know at least one person, then, when we start school."

"Oh, hey, I'll introduce you around. There's a whole bunch of us that hang around together. Do you like to swim? I'll go ask Mom if there's enough room for you to come with us this afternoon. Be right back."

Stacy glanced over the selection of books while Jill was gone. Most of the titles were fairly recent, and there were even a few she hadn't read. She picked out a couple, then glanced up at the big quilt that hung on the wall above.

It was apparently very old and somewhat tattered,

and it was enclosed in a glass display case. A little typed card read, "Friendship Quilt presented to Martha Anne Hardwicke on the occasion of her marriage to Thomas Gardner, 1774."

Stacy gasped. Martha Hardwicke! That was the girl from the cave—the one that had left the note with the corn!

Jill returned. "It's all set. Your mom says you can come."

"Great," replied Stacy. "Do you know anything about this quilt?"

"Oh, that? That's a friendship quilt. Back in the olden days when a girl got married, all her friends made a block of a quilt, then they joined them together. That one belonged to Martha Gardner. She was one of the earliest settlers, and the town was named for the mill that her family owned."

"Gardner. That's your last name too. Are you related?"

"Yup. This whole place is infested with Gardners and Harpers and Millers. We're all related somehow. It's nice to meet someone who isn't a cousin three times removed or the niece of somebody's brother-in-law."

Stacy grinned. "I can count my cousins on one hand. Do you know anything more about Martha Gardner?"

"Just that she was a prominent citizen way back in the beginning of the town. Actually, my aunt could tell you more. She's writing a history of Gardner's Mills, and she has all kinds of stuff about Martha. Are you some kind of history freak or something?" Jill said, frowning.

"No, don't worry." Stacy laughed. "I just never lived where there were so many old houses and families before."

"Come on, Stace!" called her mother. "We'd better go find your bathing suit."

"See you later," said Stacy as they headed for the door.

"Yeah, one o'clock," called Jill.

All the way home, Stacy sat deep in thought.

"What's wrong?" asked her mother.

"Oh, nothing. I was just wondering what the girls wore to swim in back in Colonial days."

Her mother said nothing, but her raised eyebrows showed surprise. From temper tantrums about leaving New Jersey to Colonial girls all in one morning was more than she could keep up with.

At a little past one o'clock, a van pulled in at the Adamses' house. Stacy called a quick good-bye to her mother and ran out just as Jill opened the door for her. The van was crammed with kids. Jill called out their names for Stacy, who promptly forgot them. She felt unusually awkward and tongue-tied, but the rest of the gang more than made up for her silence. By the time they got to the rec center, Stacy thought she had them sorted out, except for two boys who were twins.

They pulled up at a guardhouse, where the attendant waved them through. After Mrs. Gardner parked, the whole gang piled out and raced off. Jill and Stacy remained behind to help Mrs. Gardner with the gear.

They carried a large cooler between them.

"Now, which one is Jason and which is Joe?" asked Stacy.

"Jason's the one with the darker hair. He's got the neon green shorts on. You can always tell Joe 'cause he's the one Shelley is hanging around with. They've been going steady since sixth grade." She changed the subject. "That's a really cool swimsuit you have on."

"Thanks. You know, your suit is just like my friend Nikki's. Did you get it in New Jersey?"

"Actually, I got it at the mall just outside of town. Is Nikki your best friend?"

"Yeah," said Stacy. "I really miss her."

"I know what you mean. My best friend moved to Colorado last year."

They had come to a large grassy area that was dotted with blankets and sunbathers. Jill looked around.

"I guess this is okay," she said, setting down her end of the cooler. "Everybody else already piled their towels here." Mrs. Gardner joined them and set up a large beach umbrella.

"This is a nice place," said Stacy, looking around. "Pretty lake. Where's the pool?"

"Pool?" asked Jill. "There's no pool here. This is a lake."

"You mean you swim in the lake?" said Stacy. "It's green!"

"Well, yeah, it always is," said Jill. "Don't tell me you've never been swimming in a lake before!"

Stacy shifted uncomfortably. She turned to Mrs.

Gardner for support, but she was already sitting under the umbrella, her nose in a book.

"No, I've never been in a lake," she admitted finally. "W-what about seaweed and stuff?"

"Oh, don't worry," said Jill, pulling her to the water's edge. "See, there's a nice sandy bottom, and all the fish are over on the other side of the lake."

Stacy stood ankle deep in the water, still unsure.

"Pretend it's the ocean," said Jill. "You've been in the ocean, haven't you?"

"In New Jersey? Are you kidding?" said Stacy. "No way!"

"Well, suit yourself," said Jill, wading in. "You can always go sit with Mom."

Stacy hung her head and watched as Jill ran out and then dove under the water. She surfaced and swam out to a floating dock, where the rest of her gang were already taking turns on a diving board.

Stacy took a deep breath and looked out at the water. She could see the bottom, so maybe it wasn't too bad. Then she saw a flash of movement as a school of minnows darted by her legs.

"Eeek!" She jumped back. But just then Joe and Shelley came splashing up to her.

"What's wrong? Water too cold for you?" asked Joe.

"Oh, no," said Shelley. "Don't tell me you just got a new perm and can't get it wet! What a pity."

"Well, no, not exactly," stammered Stacy.

"Well, what are you waiting for? Come on," they said, pulling her into the water. "The water's great!"

Stacy allowed herself to be dragged along until she was finally wet, but her heart beat wildly nevertheless. "I'm going to get bitten by snakes and fish," she thought miserably. "Or tangled in seaweed." But nothing so dire occurred, and by the time she reached the dock, her panic had eased.

She climbed up the ladder. In New Jersey, she had been on the local diving team, so she stepped up to the board brightly. She may be a scaredy-cat, but at least she could show these guys a few moves they'd never seen before!

The next morning Stacy packed a knapsack with candles, matches, books, writing paper and pen, and a flashlight. She grabbed an old pillow and made her way to the cave. Once inside, she lit candles and made herself comfortable against the wall with the pillow and began to write a letter to Nikki, her best friend.

"Dear Nik," she began. "You'll never guess what I found—a cave of my very own!"

Stacy looked up from her letter at the shadows dancing on the wall. Somehow the words wouldn't come today. She picked up her book, but her eyes kept returning to the flickering candle-lit patterns on the wall. The peacefulness of the cave stole through her.

"This place is really neat," she thought. "I wish I had a friend to bring here." She turned her attention back to her letter, tore it up, and began again.

"Dear Nik," she wrote. "Sure do miss you and the gang." She continued her letter with an embroidered version of the bat episode, but somehow she couldn't bring herself to mention her cave.

When she had finished her letter, she lifted the pot down from its niche and reread Mattie's letter. She ran her fingers through the corn.

"I wonder if this corn would grow after being in the cave so long?" she thought. "I don't think it would be stealing to take some of it. Maybe I could find out how to grow it like Mattie did." She scooped a large handful of the seeds into her knapsack and replaced Mattie's letter. She put the pot on the ledge and tidied up her cave. She left several candles, the matches, and the pillow behind, crawled out the opening, and headed for home.

Stacy had just returned to the house when Jill called. "You want to come over? We're going to work in the garden and plant corn."

Stacy looked at her mother, who was busily gathering up paint cans and rollers and brushes.

"Please, can I go over to Jill's?" she pleaded.

"Well, I was hoping you'd help me paint," sighed her mother. "But friends are more important," she said with a smile. "Go ahead—the painting will keep."

Stacy wheeled her bike out of the old shed and pedaled down the dirt road to Jill's house. Jill met her halfway so she wouldn't miss it.

The Gardners lived in an old farmhouse that looked very much like Stacy's new home, but it was in better repair. It was a large house, surrounded by barns and sheds. There was a chicken yard, and chickens and ducks strutted and waddled about. A hutch held several rabbits, and there seemed to be dogs everywhere. Stacy was overwhelmed by the animal population.

"These are my brother's sheep," explained Jill. "He's in 4-H, and he shows them at the fair. The chickens are dinner, and the rest of the animals are pets."

"Gee," said Stacy. "I just have a couple of fish."

The girls walked over to the large garden where Jill's mother and younger brothers and sisters were busy. Jill introduced Stacy to them and showed her where to start. Most of the garden was already planted with a variety of vegetables. The corn was the last to be planted.

Stacy watched carefully as Jill showed her where to place the yellow kernels. She wanted to remember just what to do when she planted her own Indian corn.

They worked the rest of the morning and finished by lunchtime. During lunch, the phone rang and Mrs. Gardner answered.

"Sure, I'd be delighted," she said after a few moments. "No problem. See you."

She hung up the phone and turned to the girls. "I have to go out for a while. You girls are in charge. Make sure the little ones do their chores. If I'm not back by four, start the chicken, okay?" With that, she left, pausing only to smile brightly at Stacy.

"Now what was that all about?" asked Jill as Stacy shrugged.

They spent the afternoon supervising the younger children and listening to tapes and talking nonstop. By the end of the day, they discovered they were kindred spirits, agreeing on everything but their favorite colors and their chosen careers. Stacy liked blue and wanted to be a fashion designer while Jill's color was green, as was only proper for an aspiring biologist.

Mrs. Gardner returned and invited Stacy to stay for dinner. The chicken was delicious, but Stacy kept seeing and hearing the chickens clucking outside. Somehow, it just wasn't the same as eating supermarket chicken.

When Stacy got home, she found her mother sitting with her feet up.

"Have a good time?" asked Mrs. Adams.

"Yeah, sure did. Boy, do you look tired."

"Well, I certainly didn't sit around watching the soaps all day," she said as she followed Stacy up the stairs.

Stacy walked into her bedroom and stopped in her tracks. It was a miracle! The whole room had been transformed. The peeling paint was now a glistening white, with pastel satin stripe wallpaper on the walls. Pale blue curtains hung at the windows, matching the brand-new floral bedspread. The floor was covered with a thick gray pile wall-to-wall carpet. And to top it off, right on the nightstand stood a brand-new telephone of her very own!

"Oh, Mom, it's beautiful!" She threw her arms around her mother. "I don't believe it! How did you get it done so fast?"

"Kathy Gardner came and helped me this afternoon.

Do you like it?"

"Like it? I love it! You even put in a new light fixture," she said as she darted around the room. She kicked off her sneakers to sink her toes in the carpet.

"I'm glad you like it, hon," said her mother. "Now I'm going to go indulge in a nice old-fashioned soak in my old-fashioned bathtub. I feel muscles I never even knew I had!"

When her mother had gone, Stacy threw herself onto the bed. She picked up the phone and dialed Jill. How nice it was to have a new friend on the other end of the line!

The next day Stacy bounded out of bed. She hurried through breakfast and was out the door before her mother could start making ominous noises about painting. She found an old rusty spading fork in one of the old sheds and set to work digging a garden spot for her corn.

The ground was soft as she plunged in the fork, and when she turned over the rich, dark earth, she saw several worms go scurrying out of sight. She grimaced at the slimy creatures but kept on digging.

Soon she had a small plot of bare earth, two blisters, and sore shoulders. But she was satisfied and smugly smoothed her garden with an old rake.

She returned to the house for her knapsack with the corn in it. Her mother was rinsing a paintbrush at the kitchen sink.

"What are you doing out there?" she asked.

"I'm planting a garden," replied Stacy.

"A garden?" her mother asked faintly.

"Yeah, a garden. I know, I know, don't say it," Stacy said. "But you do want me to be a Vermonter, don't you?"

Her mother grinned. "Shall I get you a load of manure?"

Stacy wrinkled her nose. "Honestly, Mom, let's not go overboard," she replied, and made her exit.

The summer days drifted by for Stacy. She helped her mother paint and wallpaper, and she tended her tiny garden, where little green shoots of corn appeared almost magically. She visited her cave almost every day to read, write letters, or just daydream.

The more time she spent in the cave, the more she felt she belonged there. She had never felt that way before, not even in her plush air-conditioned New Jersey home. Here in the cave, her life took on a new perspective, and even the aching homesickness she sometimes felt vanished in the tranquility of the stone walls.

She often thought of her friends back in New Jersey, but as the days passed she missed them less and less. Her friendship with Jill grew closer, and she also began to feel accepted by Jill's friends. There were many visits to the lake with the gang, and each time Stacy found herself more comfortable, even when the weeds brushed against her legs.

Stacy sometimes started to tell Jill about her cave, but

the words just never seemed to come out, and Stacy kept it a secret.

One afternoon she and Jill went down to Gardner's Mills while Jill's mother worked in the library for a few hours. They walked all over the town, and Jill pointed out friends' houses and local landmarks. They stopped in front of a large white Colonial house that dominated the village green. Thomas Gardner had built it in 1774 to house his new bride, and subsequent generations had added on and remodeled until it rambled out in every direction. A twentieth-century Gardner had installed modern plumbing and electrical wiring, but it was large and drafty and expensive to heat. Miss Margaret Pauline Gardner now occupied it, but she was in the process of turning it into a museum.

"My Aunt Maggie lives here," said Jill. "Let's see if she's home."

Stacy agreed readily. She had already heard a lot about Aunt Maggie from Jill. She was the Gardner family's favorite aunt, always ready with a plate of cookies and a sympathetic ear. She was also the town historian, and Stacy looked forward to meeting her and actually seeing Mattie's house.

The front door was unlocked, and Jill walked right into the house, calling, "Aunt Maggie, Aunt Maggie!"

As Stacy entered behind her, she felt as if she were stepping back in time. The front room was furnished exactly as it would have been two hundred years before. Lace curtains fluttered at an open window, wafting the scent of lavender throughout the room. It was perfect, right down to the white cat curled up in the old rocking chair.

"This is neat," said Stacy, as Jill smiled.

"Yeah, I always feel like I'm right back in the olden days when I come. Aunt Maggie's been working on this place for years, gathering all the right stuff."

"It's just how I pictured Mattie's house would look," said Stacy.

"I'm so pleased to hear that," said a voice behind her, and Stacy spun around.

It was unmistakably Aunt Maggie, complete with white hair and piercing blue eyes. She wore sensible brown shoes, a tweed skirt, and a white cardigan sweater, and she carried a basket of flowers in her hand.

"Hello, Jillian dear," she said, hugging Jill. "So nice of you to drop by. And this is . . . ?"

"This is Stacy Adams. Her folks bought the old Brooks place."

"Oh, yes." Aunt Maggie smiled at Stacy. "Let's see, you're from New Jersey, aren't you? I'd recognize the accent anywhere. You girls come along in here, and we'll have tea."

"Tea?" thought Stacy. "I really am in another time."

As they followed Aunt Maggie down the hall to the kitchen, Jill said, "What did you mean when you said this is just how you pictured Mattie's house?"

Stacy flushed under Jill's puzzled gaze. "I've been seeing things all over town about Mattie. You know, that quilt in the library, and then my parents took me to lunch at the Old Grist Mill restaurant. There's a plaque there that tells all about how the Gardners built the mills and the town and everything."

Aunt Maggie came to her rescue. "That's right. It's impossible to live here in Gardner's Mills and not hear all about Mattie Gardner."

Stacy was relieved that this apparently satisfied Jill. She kicked herself mentally for the slip of her tongue. How could she explain her interest in Mattie without appearing to be a "history freak" in Jill's eyes? Or without telling her about the cave?

Aunt Maggie busied herself with the tea. Stacy was slightly disillusioned by the completely modern kitchen and was shocked to see Aunt Maggie heat the water in a microwave oven and use tea bags. But the appearance of a delicate tea service reassured her.

They carried the tea tray to the front room and settled themselves on chairs. Stacy sat up very straight and noticed that even Jill balanced her teacup very daintily.

"Martha Gardner was what you might call a found-ress," said Aunt Maggie, continuing the conversation. "She was the force behind almost every civic function when the town was developing. Her husband was the owner of the sawmill and grist mill, and he built the foundry after the war." She sipped her tea slowly. "Fortunately, Mattie kept a journal, and I've spent the better part of a lifetime transcribing it. She wasn't much of a speller, but she would have made a wonderful writer."

"She must have been a very interesting person," said Stacy.

"She certainly led an interesting life, and she was in a position to get things done because Thomas was the chief employer and businessman in the area. She had a new school built, and the old town hall. She even formed a theatrical society."

Aunt Maggie told them stories of the early days of the town, and as the girls took their leave, they made plans to return and read some of Mattie's journals.

As they walked the short block to the library to meet Jill's mother, Jill said, "I never realized how interesting things must have been back then. We always thought Aunt Maggie was a little nuts about her historical stuff, but now I'd like to read Mattie's journal."

"Yeah," agreed Stacy. "And to think that all that stuff really happened. I wonder"—she giggled as they climbed into Jill's van—"what Thomas Gardner really looked like. I wonder if he was cute."

The next morning Stacy awoke suddenly. She had had several disturbing dreams about the cave. First she dreamed she dropped the pot, shattering it beyond repair. The corn cascaded to the floor, but try as she might, she never quite managed to pick it all up. Then she decided to paint the designs of the carvings onto a sheet of paper, but no matter how hard she tried to be neat, the paint kept splashing up onto the carvings until they looked utterly destroyed. This last dream was so vivid that she rushed through breakfast and ran down to the gorge to make sure her cave was still safe and sound.

Once inside, she breathed a sigh of relief. Everything looked fine, and she sank onto her pillow to let her hammering heart slow down. "Relax," she told herself. "After all, nothing's happened to it since 1769."

She lit a candle and waited for the peaceful atmosphere of the cave to clear her mind as it always had before. It didn't work this time, though, and she got up and paced around restlessly. It didn't make sense. Why was she so worried about the cave? She looked at the carvings searchingly, as if the figures there could tell her the answer.

As she stared at the wall she remembered all the times she had started to tell Jill about the cave but never had. Then she thought of Aunt Maggie spending her entire life studying about Martha Hardwicke and Gardner's Mills without seeing Mattie's letter or the pot of corn. The more she thought about it, the more convinced she finally became that she must tell someone about the cave. Keeping the cave a secret would be as selfish as deliberately splashing paint on the walls.

"I'll tell Jill," she thought. "Even if it means this won't be my special secret place anymore."

Coming to this decision, she suddenly felt as if a burden had fallen from her shoulders. She took a deep breath, blew out the candle, and hurried up the rocks.

Jill was amazed to hear of the existence of a cave on the creek. "We've played along this creek all our lives," she said later as Stacy led her down the boulders. "Of course, we always stayed farther upstream, near my house."

Jill's amazement turned to awe as she wriggled into the opening. "To think this was here all these years!" she said as she played her flashlight over the walls. "We found some arrowheads once when we were little, so we've always figured there were Indians around at one time. But this is fantastic!"

Stacy showed her the pot of corn. She read Mattie Hardwicke's letter out loud to Jill, who sat open-mouthed.

"Wow, and to think you found this your first day here! You know, Aunt Maggie would give her eyeteeth to see this. She used to tell us that she'd give us a reward if we ever found a hidden cave."

"She knew about this cave?"

"Yeah, I guess she heard about it somewhere. There have always been rumors about a secret Indian burial ground or something."

"Could this be it?"

"Could be. It must have been hidden for a long time. I would never have guessed it was here. You really can't see it at all from outside, except from that boulder. What a neat hideout."

"Should we tell Aunt Maggie?" asked Stacy.

"We probably should," replied Jill. "She'll know who to contact."

"Contact? What do you mean?"

"Someone's going to have to come in and study this," replied Jill. "These are very old carvings, and that pot must be Indian."

"Yeah, but I'd hate to see a bunch of people come around here and start messing it up. It's so peaceful here, and I don't think it's meant to be crawled over and poked at—know what I mean?"

"I do, but this could be important. Let's talk to Aunt

Maggie and see what she says."

"I suppose you're right. It's hard, though. I feel like I want to keep the cave to myself." Stacy sighed. "I'm glad I decided to tell you about it, though."

The two girls smiled at each other. "I'm glad too," said Jill. "Don't worry, Aunt Maggie will know what to do."

Stacy's mother dropped them off at the old Gardner house, and the girls ran up the walk.

"Aunt Maggie, are you home?" Jill called out, barging through the door.

"Yes, Jillian, come right in," came Aunt Maggie's reply. "I'm in the kitchen."

Stacy and Jill joined her, and very soon the tea appeared—iced this time and garnished with a sprig of mint. Stacy, unsure of how to break the news of the cave, chattered about the weather, and Jill glanced at her several times with raised eyebrows. Finally she poked Stacy in the side with her spoon.

"Okay, okay!" Stacy glared at Jill as Aunt Maggie looked at her, puzzled. "Did Mattie Hardwicke ever mention finding anything unusual around here? Like an Indian burial ground or something like that?"

Aunt Maggie replied, "Well, yes, she mentioned an Indian cave quite often. It's funny you should ask, because I just transcribed a piece about it the other day. I've looked and looked for the cave over the years, but I've never found it, and then the doctor told me not to climb around so much anymore."

"I remember you used to offer us a reward if we found anything," said Jill.

"Yes, but no one ever did. I suppose it must have gotten buried by a rock slide."

"Could we read what she said about it?" asked Stacy.

"Of course," said Aunt Maggie. She walked to the back of the house and returned a moment later holding a piece of paper. "The part that I just finished is right here. I must say I never understood it. She wrote it just after she lost two young children to a fever." She began reading. "'I sought refuge in the cave and finally found peace and comfort. Now I know what the pictures are. Now I know the loss of the Indian girl and how she also found comfort in the cave. The raindrops are tears, and mine are finally gone, mingling in the dust with hers.'"

Stacy swallowed. Now she knew what the pictures meant. "How would you like to see the cave?" she asked in a low voice.

Aunt Maggie stared at her. "So you've found it. I should have known when you started asking questions. Where is it?"

"Down in the gorge behind our house," replied Stacy.

"The old Brooks place. Of course!" she exclaimed. "That was the original Hardwicke homestead. Well, well, well. And to think it exists after all. Are there pictures carved on the walls?"

"Yes. And there's a letter that Mattie wrote in a clay pot. I could take you there if you like," said Stacy.

"I can't wait!" said Aunt Maggie. "I don't care if I do break a leg getting to it, it will be well worth it!"

The three made plans for the next morning, and Stacy and Jill left.

"I have never seen her so excited in my life!" said Jill. "She acted like a kid at Christmas!"

Stacy nodded. "Yeah, I thought she was going to hug me to death. I'm glad we told her."

"It will be fun to show it to her," said Jill.

Stacy agreed, but deep down she felt a pang of regret. She somehow knew that her wonderful secret place just wouldn't be the same anymore.

That evening Stacy told her parents about the cave. In the lingering summer twilight, they all climbed down the boulders and explored it.

"So this is where you've been spending so much time," said Mrs. Adams.

"This is really neat," said her father. "I can understand your wanting it to be secret, but I think your friend is right. It must be hard to find pots that are hundreds of years old in such good shape."

"Probably the cool, dry air helped keep everything preserved," said her mother.

As the three climbed back up the gorge, Stacy's parents discussed the cave, talking about archaeologists and antiquities and scientific studies. Stacy didn't want to listen—all she could think was that her cave of refuge was now just something else to be studied by scientists.

The following morning a little sports car zoomed up the drive to the Adamses' house. Stacy was astonished to see Aunt Maggie and Jill climb out. Gone were Aunt

Maggie's tweed skirt and sensible shoes. She wore neon green and black hiking boots with tight blue jeans and a loud flannel shirt, with a hot pink and purple backpack slung over one arm. In her hand she carried an elaborately carved walking stick.

"This is the frail old lady you went to see?" asked Stacy's mother in an undertone as they went down the steps to meet her.

Introductions were made, but Aunt Maggie was anxious to be off, so they left. "Be sure and stop in for coffee when you get back!" called out Stacy's mother as they headed into the woods.

Stacy led the way, with Aunt Maggie close behind. "I've been up and down this creek many times and never found a thing," said Aunt Maggie.

"Well, the cave is only visible from this boulder," said Stacy. "And with this bush in front, it's really hard to see."

"I guess it takes a newcomer to see things with fresh eyes," said Aunt Maggie.

"Or maybe it was just fate," added Jill from behind.

Aunt Maggie needed no help crawling into the cave. As Jill followed her in, she stood up and flicked on her flashlight. Stacy and Jill watched silently as she flashed her light around the cave. She stepped up to the rock drawings and traced them slowly with her fingers. When she came to the pot in the niche, she examined it minutely for some time. She held Mattie's note with trembling hands.

"You know, she wrote later in her journal that right

after she wrote this letter, she met Polly. Polly Harper was her best friend for all her life. So her wish really was answered."

"I'm getting chills down my back," said Jill.

"The day after I found this cave I met Jill," said Stacy.

"Now I'm really getting chills down my back. Maybe there's a spell on this cave or something," said Jill.

"Whatever the case may be," said Aunt Maggie, "this is certainly a special place. I'm thrilled to finally be able to see Mattie's cave! She used to come here quite a bit, especially when something was bothering her, like in the passage I read you yesterday. She said the cave always made things seem clearer somehow."

"Just like me," thought Stacy. "She must have loved this place too."

Aunt Maggie produced a camera from her backpack and snapped several pictures of the pot and the carvings on the walls.

"I'll get copies of these pictures made for all of us," she said. "And I have to call the state archaeologist. She'll probably want to contact your parents, Stacy, to set up a meeting."

Stacy nodded.

The three quietly left and began the ascent up the side of the gorge. Halfway up, Aunt Maggie suddenly chuckled.

"I have a friend who claims that the Abenaki absolutely never ever made any kind of rock carvings at all," she said. "Now I can really take the wind out of his sails."

"Haven't they ever found any other carvings?" asked Stacy.

"There are a few farther south, but some say a different nation made them. These are the first this far north."

"I hope all these scientists don't turn the cave into an exhibit or something," said Stacy. "I know the Indian girl wouldn't want that."

Aunt Maggie patted her on the arm. "I'm sure the people who come to study it will be very careful not to destroy it. In fact, by letting them study it, you are ensuring that the cave will always be preserved."

They all had coffee and hot chocolate with Mrs. Adams when they got back to the house. Aunt Maggie regaled them with stories of local characters, past and present. Mrs. Adams wiped tears of laughter from her eyes. "There were certainly some original people that settled here," she said.

"Actually, it's the same all over. Every little town across this country has a story to tell. Once you start digging into the past, you find out so much about the people and the things they did, it gets addictive."

"I would like to hear more of Mattie's journal," said Jill.

Aunt Maggie nodded. "Mattie Gardner was one of a large number of women and men who were the driving force behind the formation of our country. Every community had someone like her, but unfortunately most remain nameless. Mattie is an exception because she happened to leave a journal. But I'm starting to sound like a lecturer again." She set down her cup and rose to leave. "I must get back to town, but you girls can stop by tomorrow, and we'll take a look at that journal."

As she was going out the door, she pressed a bill into Stacy's hand. "Here's that reward I offered all those years ago. You certainly have earned it."

Stacy looked at the money in her hand. One hundred dollars! She stared wide-eyed at Jill, whose mouth popped open, but the sports car roared off before she could thank Aunt Maggie.

Stacy fingered the crisp bill. "I suppose I should put it in the bank," she said. Then she looked at Jill again, and both girls burst out laughing.

"Well, maybe not all of it," Stacy said. "Mom! Can you drive us to the mall?"

The next day Stacy and Jill visited Aunt Maggie. She took them into the book-lined study at the back of the house and showed them the journal she had so carefully transcribed. Martha Hardwicke Gardner had begun keeping a journal when she was sixteen, and for the next seventy-odd years she had recorded every daily event in the life of Gardner's Mills. Her leather-bound volumes recorded births, deaths, marriages, town gossip, and even such details as the dairy cow's milk output, quarts of jelly made, and how many board feet the sawmill produced.

Stacy and Jill spent the whole day thumbing through the transcript that Aunt Maggie had prepared.

"Listen to this," said Stacy. "'June 18, 1778. Polly and

I visited Pa's cabin yesterday. It sure was sad to see it, with Ma dead these two years and Pa off fighting in the war. On our way home we saw raiders coming, so we took the babies and high-tailed it to the cave for the night. We had to leave the horses on the ridge and they got them. Polly said they were local Indians, but Gramps swore to me the last time that his band wasn't doing the thieving. Johnny thought this was a great adventure, but Polly's Joshua slept through it all.'"

The girls read how Mattie had borne seven children and lost two of them to a fever. The cave provided her a refuge in her grief then, and again many years later when her adored husband Tom was killed in a mill accident. They read how she kept the family business going until her oldest son took over.

They chuckled when they read, "'This evening Elizabeth'"—her grown daughter—"'took me to a lecture at the town hall. There was some so-called expert and he claimed there were never any Indians here in the Green Mountains. The old goat! I wanted to speak up and tell him about Gramps and his Indian clan, but Elizabeth pinched me and told me not to go about blabbing all the family scandals. Didn't I raise that girl to have any respect for her elders? Scandal, indeed!'"

Stacy and Jill rose reluctantly to leave.

"I'll have the rest of the journal finished in a few weeks," said Aunt Maggie.

"Oh, good," said Jill. "I can't wait to see how it turns out!"

"Now who's the history freak?" asked Stacy.

"Me!" retorted Jill, and both girls laughed as they ran out the door.

The archaeologist called Mrs. Adams and set up a meeting for the following week.

"Next week," said Stacy, writing the date on the calendar. "And then just two more weeks, and school starts!" She stuck out her tongue. "Just when I was starting to have fun too."

Jill's family went to Maine for a week. Stacy moped around the house until her mother finally said, "How would you like to go to New Jersey for the weekend?"

Stacy's eyes lit up. "Would I ever! I can't wait to go home!"

But the weekend was a little disappointing. It was nice to see her old friends, but she didn't really feel like one of the gang anymore. Even she and Nikki didn't seem to be able to talk the way they used to. The old neighborhood overflowed with buildings and people, and Stacy felt hemmed in by the traffic and the crowds. Even the mall, her old hangout, seemed noisy and crowded. Her mother was surprised to find her packed and ready to go back to Vermont ahead of time.

Stacy herself was amazed to find that she was actually glad to see the green "Welcome to Vermont" sign as they drove back home. She noticed that the bright greens of summer were fading to golds and oranges. The next morning there was a decided nip in the air as she rode down to Jill's house.

The girls spent the morning comparing vacations, but soon the talk turned to school. Stacy couldn't decide whether she was excited or just plain scared to death.

"Don't worry," said Jill. "You know a bunch of people already. You'll fit in fine."

As Stacy turned into her driveway that afternoon, she saw a strange car. The state archaeologist! She hurriedly put her bike in the shed and ran into the house, hearing voices in the kitchen.

Conversation ceased as she ran into the room.

"Oh, here's Stacy now," said her mother as Stacy stared at the people sitting around the table.

"Stacy, this is Joanne Nelson, the state archaeologist, and this is Dr. Landers from the university. And this is Rick Dupree. He's a graduate student at the university, but he's also representing the Abenaki nation."

Stacy looked the three over. She had rather expected bespectacled men in long white coats with huge magnifying glasses, but all three looked quite normal. Ms. Nelson was a tall blonde in her thirties, Dr. Landers was an older gentleman, and Rick Dupree was young, with a definite twinkle in his dark eyes. Stacy found herself returning their smiles.

"So this is our treasure-finder," said Dr. Landers. "Pleased to meet you, Stacy. I'm very anxious to see this cave. Shall we go?"

All three shouldered backpacks and they started off, with Stacy leading the way. Dr. Landers questioned her

extensively all the way to the cave. His enthusiasm was catching, and Stacy warmed to him immediately.

"So you actually slipped and fell onto this rock," he said. "Hmmm. I certainly wouldn't have noticed a cave here. It's well hidden." He rummaged in his backpack and fished out a large flashlight. "I can't tell you what a tremendous find this is. Lead the way!"

The three followed Stacy into the cave, and the tiny cave was suddenly filled with light as they all switched on flashlights. There was a stunned silence from the group.

"Would you look at those carvings," breathed Ms. Nelson.

"Amazing!" said Dr. Landers. "Definitely stone chiseled, I'd say," he pronounced peering through a large magnifying glass. He launched into an impromptu lecture on the carvings, discussing lines and angles and so forth.

Rick Dupree stepped up to the niche and gingerly withdrew the pot. He examined it minutely before he even opened it.

"It's Abenaki, all right," he said. "You can see how it was formed by hand, then etched with a carved wooden roller. The clay isn't local, though. I'd say it was made farther north and then carried here."

Dr. Landers broke off his dissertation on the carvings and hurried over.

"I would have to agree with you on that," he said. "Notice the design and the spaces between the lines."

Rick produced a notebook and started taking notes while Dr. Landers and Ms. Nelson took pictures. They measured the cave and drew sketches.

Stacy remained by the opening, feeling very lost and overwhelmed. Occasionally one of the adults asked her a question, but for the most part she remained silent. Finally Rick looked up from his note taking and smiled.

"You must think we're nuts," he said.

"No, not at all. I just never thought my cave was this important."

"It's one of the best finds in Vermont," he said. "It's not particularly old, but because everything is intact, it's very valuable, especially to the Abenaki. And it's very valuable for more than just the scientific impact."

"What do you mean?"

"Judging from the carvings and the pot of corn, I'd say this was meant to be a burial chamber. There are no actual bodies buried here, but it may have been meant to be a place of refuge in the afterlife. That makes it a sacred place, one that must be preserved for our people."

Stacy nodded. "What will happen to the cave?"

"I'll meet with the members of our council and the decision will be theirs. I am going to personally recommend that they let us take records and make a latex impression." Rick glanced at Stacy's bewildered expression. "We paint the cave walls with latex and let it dry. Then we peel it off and get a perfect impression of the wall without damaging it. Then we make our own copy of the cave wall in the lab and study it without disturbing the cave itself," he explained.

"Oh, I see," said Stacy. "And after you make the impression?"

"I'll recommend that the cave be left alone."

Stacy's spirits rose. "You mean, just leave it alone?"

"I would like it left alone, but the decision is not mine to make."

Rick turned back to his note taking, and Stacy continued to watch them work. What a relief to know that he didn't want to turn the cave into a scientific exhibit!

Ms. Nelson called her over. "Show me exactly how the pot stood in the niche," she said. Stacy placed it on the ledge as well as she could remember and stepped back as Ms. Nelson snapped a photo.

"I wonder if any of this corn would germinate after all these years," said Ms. Nelson.

"Actually, it did pretty well," said Stacy. "About half of it came up."

"You mean you planted some?" Ms. Nelson said in surprise.

"Well, yes. I thought it would be okay," said Stacy. "I only took a handful."

"That's all right," said Dr. Landers. "You left plenty for us to study. And you say it actually came up? The ag fellows will probably be interested in your crop. Remind me to take a look at it when we leave."

The three finally decided they had done enough for a preliminary report, and they gathered their equipment and left. Stacy led them back up the boulders while Dr. Landers snapped pictures on the way.

Stacy showed them her garden, where her corn stood tall. The ears of corn were somewhat smaller than the corn in Jill's garden, but the darkening cornsilk indicated that it would soon be ripe.

"I'm surprised it came up at all," said Dr. Landers. "But I suppose the Abenakis would have bred it for its keeping qualities."

They said good-bye and drove off. Stacy and her

mother stood on the porch and watched them leave.

"So what's next?" asked her mother. "Wait and see what the Abenaki council decides to do?"

"Yeah," said Stacy. "I guess it's up to them."

The day before school started, Stacy and Jill and the gang went to the lake one last time. The grassy bank was almost deserted, and the summer houses around the lake's edge all wore an abandoned, boarded-up look.

Stacy shivered as she climbed out of the water.

"Brrr!" she said. "It's warmer in the water."

"Won't be for long," said Joe as he handed her a toasted marshmallow.

"Just think," said Shelley, "in a few months this lake will be frozen hard enough to drive on, and we'll be skating right where we swam today."

"That I have to see," said Stacy. "I can't imagine driving on a lake—but then, when I first came here, I couldn't imagine swimming in one either."

Shelley grinned. "I guess you've come a long way." The gang laughed as she added, "Before long, you'll even be saying 'yup' and 'cold 'nough fer ya,' just like a real Vermonter."

"Yup," said Stacy, laughing along with the rest of her friends.

Stacy's mother met her at the door when she got home that evening.

"Rick Dupree called. The council decided to allow Dr. Landers to make records and his latex impression, then

they want the cave left alone. Someone from the Abenaki will come from time to time to visit it and make
sure it's maintained properly, but for the most part, it's
to be left as it is. Since it's on the creek there won't be
danger of it being bulldozed."

Stacy grinned. "All right! I'm really glad to hear that.
That's the best news I've heard all year!"

"I thought you'd like to hear that," said her mother.
"Rick will be by to pick up the clay pot next Saturday,
and—"

"Pick up the clay pot? But I thought you said they
were going to leave everything as it was!" cried Stacy.

"They decided the pot's just too fragile. If an animal
or a vandal happened to get in there, it could easily get
knocked to the ground and broken. You wouldn't want
them to take that chance, would you?"

"No, I suppose not." Stacy bit her lip. "But I was going
to leave a note in it for the next person, just like Mattie
did," she said softly.

Her mother thought for a moment. "I think you could
still leave a note, Stace. Just use a glass jar instead of the
clay pot."

Stacy smiled as she considered the idea. "That's great,
Mom," she said. "I could put some of my corn in it, and
a copy of Mattie's note. Jill can help me get it ready.
Now, if you'd just say I don't have to go to school tomorrow, I'd really be happy."

"Sorry," called her mother as Stacy ran upstairs to her
room, "I already told them you'd be there!"

Stacy had to admit that Jill was right about school. It wasn't too bad—in fact, she liked her classes, and she actually felt a part of things by the end of the first week.

On Saturday, Stacy was in the old shed when she heard Rick's truck drive up. She called out to him, and he joined her, carrying a large metal box.

"How's it going?" he asked.

"Good," said Stacy. "I'm fixing up a jar to put in the cave after you take the old pot away."

"That's a good idea! What are you putting in it?"

"Some of the corn, of course. And there's a copy of Mattie's letter. Jill did it with her calligraphy set. She even left in all the misspelled words. I wrote a note too. It says:

"'My name is Stacy Ann Adams, and I was born in New Jersey. I found this cave the very first day I came to Vermont. There was a pot with corn inside and the note from Martha Hardwicke. The pot was made by an Indian girl, who carved the pictures in the wall. The pot had corn in it that Mattie grew. I grew some of it, too, and that's where this corn came from. The original pot was taken by the Abenaki so it could be preserved and seen by everyone.

"'If you want to find out more about Martha Hardwicke, contact the Gardner's Mills Historical Society. She was a neat person.

"'To find out more about the cave, contact the Abenaki nation. This cave belongs to the Abenaki, and it is a sacred place. Please do not do anything to destroy it. It is very special to all of us. Sincerely, Stacy Ann Adams, September 21, 1991.'"

"That's great," said Rick. "I like this picture of you and Jill with the corn behind you."

Inside the cave, the two carefully packed the pot into the metal box, cushioning it with shredded paper. Stacy placed her jar on the ledge and knelt before it.

"It doesn't look the same," she said.

"No, it doesn't," admitted Rick. "But things hardly ever stay the same in this world."

Stacy remained silent.

Rick spoke. "You really have a thing for this cave, don't you?"

"Yes, I do," said Stacy. She looked at Rick. "You may think this is stupid, but it's the first place in my life that I've ever felt I really belonged. I lived in the same house all my life, but I never really felt I truly belonged anywhere until I found this cave. I don't ever want to lose that feeling."

"I know what you mean, actually," said Rick. "When I was about your age, I felt very confused and alone. One day I took a long hike into the forest. I walked for hours, until I was completely alone, not a sign of another human being. I sat down on a rock and became as still as I could. I put away all thoughts of my problems and life and just sat. I watched the animals and birds and trees and rocks, and slowly it dawned on me: It doesn't matter what or who we are or where we come from. We all have a place just like all the birds and animals and rocks and trees have a place. We belong to this world, together."

"Maybe that's what I'm feeling when I come here," said Stacy.

Rick nodded. "There is a very strong sense of peace here. Remember, too, that the girl who carved these pictures was of a different culture. She was very aware that she belonged to the world, not that the world belonged to her. In today's society, with everyone squabbling over what belongs to who, it's easy to forget that concept."

"Do you feel you belong anywhere?"

"I do now. That long walk made me realize that I am who I am. I am an Abenaki, with a rich heritage, and I also live in this world that is made up of many different peoples. We all have a place, and all of us have cultures and customs that are important. I want my children to grow up knowing where they come from and feeling proud of their heritage."

"I wish I had a heritage like this." Stacy motioned to the cave walls.

Rick smiled. "But you do. The heritage of these people is for all of us, not just those, like me, who share the same blood. They are Vermont's past, and so they are a part of all of us, because we are the future."

Stacy thought for a moment. "I wonder if the next person who finds this cave will have the same problems we've had."

"Probably," said Rick. "And if they do, hopefully this cave will still be a quiet place where they can sort them out."

Stacy and Rick climbed up the rocks, carefully carrying the metal box between them.

"Would you like to stay for lunch?" asked Stacy as she set down the box for a rest. "We're having the rest of my Indian corn."

"Oh, really? Did you grind it up and mix it with dried berries and venison?"

"Well, no," admitted Stacy. "My mother is going to cook the ears in the microwave."

Rick laughed. "What kind of Indian are you anyway? Now don't hit me!" he cried as Stacy swung. "I was only teasing. I'd love some nuked corn."

They picked up the box once more and turned toward home, their laughter sounding through the trees. At this strange sound, a hawk fluttered up from his perch on a high limb and wheeled toward the sky. Slowly it circled, hunting for this disturbance, until finally the noise was gone. Satisfied his territory was again safe and secure, the hawk spiraled slowly downward, down toward the falling water of the creek below.

After lunch, Stacy called Jill, and the two of them went into town to see Aunt Maggie.

She met them at the door with a triumphant smile. "I finally finished the journal," she said. "Come and read it while I make the tea."

Stacy and Jill seated themselves on the antique settle. The white cat jumped onto Stacy's lap, and she stroked it gently. Jill read aloud from the last entry.

"'November 28, 1843. Polly died today. Joshua came and got me about noon, and I went upstairs to her room.

She was lying there just as she has since she became ill, with only her left foot twitching back and forth, back and forth. I couldn't help but think back to that day we met, her with her china blue eyes and yellow hair. "My friends call me Polly," she had said. I sat there and held her hand, and then she opened her eyes for the first time since she fell. She couldn't talk but then we always knew what the other was thinking. "Good-bye, Polly," I said, and then her eyes closed. Her foot stopped twitching, and I knew she was gone. Elizabeth brought me home and put me to bed with a hot brick. I still feel chilled, and I just wish I could go to my cave. I know I'd feel better there, but I'll never get down those rocks again. I keep wondering—who will be the next person to find it? Who will it be? And will they cherish it as I have?'"

Jill closed the folder and looked out the window. Stacy stared down at the cat in her lap until Aunt Maggie bustled in with the tea. Then she sighed and picked up her cup.

"I guess I'm the one Mattie was talking about," she said. And Mattie's words echoed in her mind: "Who will be the next person to find it? Who will it be? And will they cherish it as I have?"